"Paul, we have absolutely nothing in common," Coral insisted. "We approach life from two opposite directions. We don't want the same things."

"Are you so sure about that?" he asked quietly, his gaze going to her mouth.

Coral ran her tongue over her bottom lip after he brushed the soft pad of his thumb across the small indentation made by her teeth. She didn't look away when she felt a shiver of reaction vibrate through her.

He smiled slowly. "You were saying something about not wanting the same thing. Right now I want to see if you taste as exciting as I think you will, and you're curious to know what it would be like if I kissed you."

"But you aren't going to kiss me now," she said with certainty.

"I'm not?" he asked, tilting his head slightly to one side in order to contemplate her expression. "What would stop me?"

"Time."

He blinked, clearly confused by her answer. "What about time?"

"I think that once you decide to do something, you would want to take your time doing it."

Paul closed his fingers over her slender shoulders and held her in front of him. "A very long time," he murmured softly. "Long and deep and hard, and I'm not going to wait much longer. . . ."

WHAT ARE *LOVESWEPT* ROMANCES?

They are stories of true romance and touching emotion. We believe those two very important ingredients are constants in our highly sensual and very believable stories in the LOVE-SWEPT line. Our goal is to give you, the reader, stories of consistently high quality that may sometimes make you laugh, sometimes make you cry, but are always fresh and creative and contain many delightful surprises within their pages.

Most romance fans read an enormous number of books. Those they truly love, they keep. Others may be traded with friends and soon forgotten. We hope that each LOVESWEPT romance will be a treasure—a "keeper." We will always try to publish

LOVE STORIES YOU'LL NEVER FORGET
BY AUTHORS YOU'LL ALWAYS REMEMBER

The Editors

Loveswept® 750

WILD IN THE NIGHT

PATT BUCHEISTER

BANTAM BOOKS
NEW YORK · TORONTO · LONDON · SYDNEY · AUCKLAND

WILD IN THE NIGHT
A Bantam Book / August 1995

If you would be interested in receiving protective vinyl covers for your
Loveswept books, please write to this address for information:

Loveswept
Bantam Books
P.O. Box 985
Hicksville, NY 11802

ISBN 0-553-44498-0

Published simultaneously in the United States and Canada

PRINTED IN THE UNITED STATES OF AMERICA

OPM   0 9 8 7 6 5 4 3 2 1

ONE

The soundproofing system Coral Bentley recommended to many of her clients worked so well in her office, she wasn't aware of the activity going on in the reception area until her door was pushed open with considerable force.

Startled, she almost dropped the spoonful of blueberry yogurt she'd been about to eat. She quickly shoved the plastic spoon into the yogurt container on her desk, barely making it before the contents spilled.

Now that she no longer had to worry about staining her white Italian-silk skirt, she gave the intruder her full attention.

The man who marched across the carpet toward her was not happy. Coral wasn't simply making a guess when she came to that conclusion. The stormy expression in his gray eyes was the most obvious indication. But when that was combined with the scowl on his tanned face and the stiff way he held himself, she didn't need a flashing neon sign above his head to announce his mood.

Furious would cover it, she decided, puzzled why anyone could be so angry on such a beautiful, sunny September day.

And apparently at her, since she was the one on the receiving end of his dark glare.

Coral could count on one hand the clients who hadn't been totally pleased with the work Quality Interior Designs did for them, but none of them had barged into her office to complain. In one case a phone call had settled the problem. In the others a quick trip to the premises had corrected the situation to everyone's satisfaction.

This occasion might prove to be the exception, she mused, although technically this man didn't fit the category of business complaints. She had met all of her clients, and he wasn't one of them. Nor could she recall ever meeting this man outside of business. She was left with the irrefutable conclusion that a complete stranger was livid with her.

"Somebody has apparently smudged your rose-colored glasses this morning," she said.

The man stopped abruptly several feet away and stared at her, a guarded expression replacing the fury in his eyes.

"Pardon?"

"You don't seem to be having a good day," she explained.

She leaned back in her chair as he approached her desk, less in a rush than he had been. In fact he was looking at her with marked caution, as though she were a stick of dynamite with a possibly faulty fuse.

He was tall, perhaps six feet in height, she guessed, although his slim, athletic frame made him appear even taller. She estimated his age to be in the early thirties, although she wasn't particularly expert at judging people's ages. He was dressed all in black, from the polished leather loafers she'd glimpsed when he stood in the doorway to the thick ebony hair that could have used a trim several weeks ago. The dark colors should have given him a somber, oppressive appearance, but instead he resembled an ad for a well-dressed businessman just returning from a vacation who hadn't had time to go to his barber yet.

When only the width of the desk separated them, Coral was able to see the blue stripes in his black shirt, which were so subdued as to be almost nonexistent.

Like his sense of humor, she thought. He undoubtedly had the ability to smile, but certainly not the inclination this morning.

Resting her elbows on the arms of her upholstered chair, Coral touched the tips of her fingers together as she contemplated her unex-

pected visitor. She felt an odd tingle of aware-
ness when his gaze met hers. He studied her
with an intensity that was disturbing in a way
she couldn't explain. She had the unsettling feeling that he could see into her soul, and she
fought an instinctive desire to look away.

His eyes were the color of wet slate, his expression intent and frankly curious. He didn't
immediately begin a tirade of complaints. He
just kept looking at her.

Coral got the impression he was taking the
time to adjust his approach, similar to the way a
hunter might when he discovered his quarry
wasn't quite what he'd expected. The analogy
was an odd one considering she was in an office
in a large building in the nation's capital, not
wandering around in a primitive forest with an
expert marksman on her trail. Whether it made
sense or not, though, the feeling of being
weighed and measured remained.

A movement behind him drew Coral's gaze
to her secretary, who was maneuvering her
wheelchair through the doorway with as much
speed as possible on the carpeted floor.

Louise Wilson's physical handicap hadn't
mattered to Coral when Louise had applied for
the job, nor had it stopped her from performing
her duties efficiently and well. A pleasant, lively
woman of thirty-one with curly reddish brown
hair and wide-spaced green eyes, Louise was
loyal, intelligent, and articulate. She could also

be outrageously outspoken when the occasion required it. And sometimes when it didn't.

"I'm sorry, Miss Bentley," she said quickly. "This man asked if you were in and he barged past my desk when I said yes. He doesn't have an appointment."

Coral smiled. "Isn't it amazing how some people feel they don't need one?"

"Do you want me to call Security?"

"Not yet, Louise. He obviously has something important to say that he feels can't wait. I'm keeping my fingers crossed that he isn't selling something. What time is my meeting with Midvale?"

"In an hour."

Shifting her gaze to the man, who was still staring at her, she asked, "Will forty-five minutes be long enough for whatever discussion you had in mind, or will you be needing more time?"

Surprise flickered in his eyes. "It depends on the answers you give me."

Coral held his gaze for a few seconds as she absorbed the fact that he spoke with a clipped, upper-class British accent. Speaking the Queen's English wasn't much of a clue to his identity, however, nor did it help explain why he'd barged into her office. She dealt with a variety of people, from diplomats and politicians to hair stylists and plumbers, in the Washington, D.C., area, and many of them spoke with an accent.

She glanced at Louise again. "Let's hope I

have the correct answers, or you'll have to call Douglas at Midvale and reschedule." When Louise made no move to leave the office, Coral nodded toward the open doorway. "It's all right, Louise. You can go back to your desk. I'll give the signal if you need to call for backup."

Louise studied the intruder thoroughly as if cataloging his features in the event she needed to describe him to a police sketch artist. Then she turned her wheelchair around and left the office.

Coral shifted her gaze back to her unexpected guest. "Would you mind introducing yourself?" She smiled. "If for no other reason than I'll have a name to give Security if the need arises."

His gaze scanned her face. "You're certainly a cool one."

He didn't make it sound like a compliment, Coral noticed. "I'm also quite busy, although it might not look like it at the moment." She snapped a lid onto the container of yogurt and dropped it and the spoon into the waste bin beside her desk. "Could you possibly get to the point some time soon?"

"What's the signal you give your secretary so that she'll send in the heavy artillery?"

So he did have a sense of humor after all, she thought, irrationally pleased by the glimpse of amusement in his eyes.

She gestured toward the phone on her desk. "I push the intercom button twice."

"Have you ever had to summon them to rescue you before?"

"Not yet," she said, wondering if this would be the first time. "There hasn't been a problem that I haven't been able to solve without sending for reinforcements. Of course there's always an exception to every rule. You obviously aren't here to present me with an award for business excellence, so would you mind getting to the reason for your impressive entrance?"

His frown was more from being puzzled than from temper. At least she hoped that was the case.

"You aren't at all as I expected," he said.

"Life is full of interesting little surprises, isn't it?" she said dryly. "Take your visit as an example."

He gave her a long, assessing look that made her want to check to make sure all of the buttons on her shirt were securely fastened. It wasn't like her to fidget, but the inclination persisted.

Her patience was fraying when he finally reached into the pocket of his shirt and withdrew a business card. Tossing it onto her desk, he said, "I'm Paul Forge. My partner, John Keats, said you're the person to talk to about the condition of my office."

She read the name Outfitters Ltd. printed on the card with his name in the upper-left corner.

"Ah," she said hesitantly.

"That's not very helpful. What does it mean?"

"'Ah' sounds better than the unladylike word that came immediately to mind."

"Why would knowing my name cause you to swear?"

She looked up at him. "What makes you think I was about to say a curse word?"

"Weren't you?"

"Maybe a little one."

"Why?"

"John Keats mentioned our work was to be a surprise to you. Am I correct in assuming the surprise was not a pleasant one?"

"It went over with a bang," he said in a wry tone.

She raised an eyebrow. "That sounds loud."

"It was. The windows in John's office are probably still vibrating."

"Well," she said, "now we're getting somewhere. Since I am the one to see about any complaints, what exactly is the problem you're having with the new system, Mr. Forge?"

He clamped his hands on his hips and glared at her. "I can't find a bloody damn thing."

Coral blinked. "The filing system we installed in each office is fairly standard, Mr. Forge. It requires knowledge of the alphabet, and if that's not a problem, you should be able to locate whatever it is you're looking for without any difficulty."

"I do know how to spell, Miss Bentley," he said with a quelling glance. "Or is it Mrs. Bentley? I dislike using that ambiguous form of Ms., but I'll manage if you insist."

"Miss will do nicely," she murmured, unconsciously copying his more formal speech pattern.

"Miss Bentley," he began politely, "I want everything put back the way it was when I left the office two weeks ago."

Coral sighed. "This morning my horoscope said I was approaching a cycle of increased activity. That's an obvious understatement."

He blinked twice. "Pardon?"

"I've had a few unusual requests since I started this business four years ago, but yours wins the prize for most bizarre, Mr. Forge. Quality Interior Design specializes in organizing messes. We don't create them. If you could be more specific about your complaint, I'm sure we can find a solution to your problem."

"I told you. I can't find anything. My office is all changed around. Someone nicked my dartboard off the wall for starters. Off the blasted wall!"

"Nicked," she repeated. She poised a pen over a pad of paper. "My staff is usually very careful. Whatever was damaged will be repaired at no cost to you. If you could give me the details, I'll arrange to have some estimates done right away."

"Nothing was damaged. Things were taken, stolen, heisted, nicked." He began to pace as he listed his grievances. "The dartboard is gone. There are two hulking filing cabinets in the way, even if the board were still there. I now have a shiny new computer on a table where the soft-drinks machine used to be." He glared at her. "That has come up missing too."

"Uh-oh," she said under her breath, but unfortunately he heard her.

"What do you mean, uh-oh?" he asked as he stopped abruptly, his hands on his hips, his eyes narrowing with suspicion.

"A dartboard and a soft-drinks machine isn't the typical office furnishings we usually deal with, and I remember seeing them. I'll check, but I'm pretty sure I know which office was yours."

"Good. We're finally getting somewhere."

Coral indicated the chair opposite her desk. "Why don't you sit down, Mr. Forge, while I look at your file?"

"It isn't necessary to waste time going through your records. My request is very simple. I want someone to undo the damage your tidy patrol did to my office."

"I can't tell exactly what was done until I see the file," she explained with as much patience as she could muster. "Would you like a cup of coffee while you wait?"

"This isn't a social call."

"Obviously." For the first time since he'd barged into her office, Coral didn't bother hiding her irritation. "Evidently it's your nature to be surly, Mr. Forge, but I've found good manners and polite behavior make even the most unpleasant experience easier to cope with. You might want to try it sometime."

"I am not surly," he said, clearly affronted by her statement.

Coral swiveled her chair so that she was facing the computer screen on her left. "Sit, stand, pace, lean against the wall, or do cartwheels if you want to, Mr. Forge. I'm still going to access the Outfitters file to determine how to fix your problem."

"I already told you. I want my office back the way it was."

"I won't know how it was, how it is now, or even which office we're talking about for sure unless I look at the files. You've had your say, and I know what you want. If you'll give me a few minutes, I'll be better prepared to tell you if we can do anything to help you find your dartboard."

Paul watched her tap on the computer keyboard, her slender fingers moving with speed and ease as she concentrated on the screen and ignored him. He had the unsettling feeling she was also humoring him. Possibly she was even silently laughing at him, although he couldn't tell from her expression.

His mouth twisted in a grimace as he sat down in the chair she'd indicated. He'd handled his entrance into Coral Bentley's office with all the finesse of a bull elephant.

His frustration and anger over the condition of his office had lasted through the verbal chewing out he'd given his partner and had continued brewing during the drive from Outfitters to the building where Quality Interior Designs was located in Alexandria. He would apologize to John when he returned to the office. He didn't regret making his feelings clear—that he disliked having his territory invaded by orderly little munchkins while he was away—but he had overreacted.

He could sympathize with his partner's confusion at his extreme behavior, in light of the fact that change was something that usually appealed to Paul. Their business of arranging trips for sportsmen provided him with a reason to travel all over the world, checking out possible locations for their clients. Consistency was not generally his strong suit. Routine drove him around the bend. He liked adventure, change, new horizons, and variety.

But not in his office. That was different. Like his family home in England, his space at Outfitters was his base, always there to return to no matter how long he stayed away. He enjoyed challenging himself, but he also liked a secure anchorage to keep himself grounded.

He had to respect his partner's timing. John had ordered the thorough cleaning, the updated computer stations, and the new filing system to be installed while Paul was away on a trip. It was sneaky, but understandable. If he had been there, no one would have been allowed to touch a single sheet of paper from the stacks piled on his desk and credenza.

Just because some of the brochures and advertisements were several years old didn't mean that there wasn't some valuable information to be gotten from them. Paul had known where each bit of correspondence was located, could have put his fingers on any facts and figures needed at any given moment. Appearances to the contrary, there had been a method to the mess.

Then Quality Interior Design had been allowed to muck about with his possessions.

He couldn't possibly do any work on a desk that was polished to such a high sheen, it nearly blinded him when he sat down. The only object left on its shiny surface was an antique pen and inkwell that had belonged to one of his illustrious ancestors, and a telephone with an astonishing array of buttons. He remembered placing the writing set on the desk when he and John started Outfitters. He hadn't seen it since.

To add to his indignation, he'd learned his precious papers were now stored in color-coded files, of all things. When he'd opened a file drawer, he saw a rainbow of pinks, yellows, and blues, their little tabs clearly labeled. A handsomely designed printed set of instructions to the files had been left in the top drawer of his desk.

Which had been invaded as well. Paper clips were in an indented tray, each one arranged identically rather than in a healthy, normal jumble. His catapult, or slingshot in American vernacular, made from a couple of pencils and rubber bands was missing. How was he supposed to shoot paper wads across the room into the wastebasket while he was working out the tricky details of a trip? Someone had even removed a supply of peppermint sweets he remembered leaving in a wadded-up white paper sack a couple of months ago.

The can of stubby pencils on his desk had been replaced by long, lethally sharpened pencils stuck into a posh brass container. He'd read somewhere that Thomas Edison had three-inch thick-lead pencils specially made for him because he preferred the shorter length. Paul did, too, but evidently the shipshape patrol thought they were tacky rather than an eccentricity of genius.

He'd learned from John that it was Quality Interior Design's organizational team that had turned his inner sanctum into a spotless show-room. If a photographer from *Better Offices and Warehouses* wanted a cover photo for their next issue, he had just the place. That was all the office was good for in its present condition. Paul couldn't actually work in such an oppressive environment.

Irritation had crowded out indignation by the time he'd arrived at the offices of Quality Interior Design, the diabolical company responsible for rendering his office sterile. He had come up with several choice things to say to whoever had sent the tidy fanatics to Outfitters.

The object of his visit was to make the person in charge send the overly trained neat-freaks back to his office to undo the damage they had done. He wanted every slip of paper, brochure, schedule, instruction manual, and map back the way it had been before he'd taken off to Minnesota to check out a fishing lodge.

Upon meeting the person in charge, though, he'd thrown out his planned speech. He was still irked by the inconvenience he'd faced when he returned, but he was also intrigued by Coral Bentley.

Paul leaned back in the chair and studied Coral while she concentrated on the computer screen. Taken one at a time, her features would have to be classified as ordinary, he thought. Her medium-brown hair was thick, shiny, and fairly short, the sides brushed toward the longer length in back in a simple, yet classy style. She wore a minimum amount of makeup, unless she was an expert at applying gobs of the stuff so that she looked like she wore very little. Growing up with a sister had taught him that women got up to all sorts of tricks to make themselves look ravishing, tricks that a mere man couldn't begin to understand.

In all honesty he couldn't say that Coral Bentley fit the ravishing category. The only word that came to mind in his extensive vocabulary of French, Spanish, and English was to describe her as average. Not that she wasn't attractive. She was, in her own way. The cool professional type usually didn't appeal to him, but she had held his attention from the moment he saw her.

His gaze narrowed as he examined her even more thoroughly. She wore a simple white silk shirt under a hip-length black vest with a wide gold necklace around her slim throat. He had caught a glimpse of a slim white skirt when he'd been standing in front of her desk, but he had no way of determining the length or the shape of her legs. His guess was that they were average.

However, his reaction to her was anything but ordinary, or even familiar.

He brought his gaze back to her face when she turned her head in his direction. "Are you serious about wanting your office returned to its former state?" she asked.

He smiled at the barely concealed disbelief in her voice. "As soon as possible."

She turned to face him completely, resting her forearms on the desk. "Why? I checked the layout of the offices just now, and I had a flashback of the first time I saw that room."

"You make it sound like the Chamber of Horrors at a wax museum."

"The sight was just as unforgettable. I remember asking Mr. Keats if the room was used for storage and if everyone stood in the doorway and simply tossed things inside."

"I imagine John thought that was quite funny."

"Now that you mention it, he did seem amused at the time." She returned her attention back to the computer. "This is interesting. According to my records," she said with a gesture toward the display screen, "it took three times as long to do your office than it did to organize all the others. That gives you some idea of how much work my staff had to do." She looked at him. "Why in the world would you want us to change everything back?"

"I liked it the way it was."

Coral glanced at the screen, which was displaying a room layout with detailed descriptions and symbols. The sheer number of codes representing what had been in a particular location was mind-boggling. She brought her gaze back to his. "I'm not sure we could duplicate the chaos, Mr. Forge. It would be like reconstructing an earthquake after the town had been rebuilt."

"It wasn't that bad."

Coral raised a skeptical eyebrow, but didn't argue the point. She reached toward the phone.

Paul leaned forward. "What are you doing?" he asked sharply.

Surprised by the sudden change from congenial to cautious, she said, "I was going to ask Louise to bring in the Outfitters' main file."

He jerked his head toward the computer. "You've been looking at the files for the last five minutes."

"We take photographs of every room before and after the work is done. Those we file away in vertical files. The other information is condensed into the computer."

Paul relaxed. Sitting back, he said, "See if you can resist pressing the intercom button twice. I'm not in the mood to be manhandled by burly security guards. This is a new shirt."

Smiling, Coral pressed the intercom button once and asked her secretary for the Outfitters' main file. When that was done, she pushed back her chair and stood.

"Are you sure you wouldn't like some coffee, Mr. Forge? It will take Louise a few minutes to get the file. I'm going to have a cup and can just as easily pour one for you."

He nodded. "Cream, no sugar."

Coral felt his gaze on her as she walked around the desk. The insulated pitcher of coffee was on one end of a long credenza about five steps away. She had never considered it much of a distance before. But then she'd never been self-conscious about anyone watching her the way Paul Forge was. Even when she turned her back toward him, she could feel the intensity of his gaze.

After she added cream as he'd requested, she walked over to his chair and held the cup and saucer out to him.

He looked up at her. "Thank you," he murmured as he took the saucer from her hand.

Puzzled by the hitch in her breathing when she met his eyes, Coral stood transfixed. The flicker of recognition was startling, yet she couldn't describe the odd sensation any other way. She had never met the man before today, so how could she feel this sense of familiarity toward him?

Before she could come up with an answer to her question, Paul spoke.

"I'm beginning to see how good you are."

"You're easily impressed," she said. "Most people can pour a cup of coffee."

"I meant your ability to put everything in its place. I didn't plan on sitting down, much less having a cup of coffee when I came here, yet I'm doing both."

"I doubt if anyone could make you do anything you didn't want to do, Mr. Forge." Remembering why he was there, she added, "Unless it was done behind your back."

Paul acknowledged her comment with a faint smile. "Which brings us back to the reason for my visit. I admit I didn't think about how much was involved with organizing office space. From what I've seen, your computer records are very thorough. Why do you need the photographs?"

"Most of the design work is done here rather than on-site. We use photographs to go with the measurements and diagrams of the floor plans to plan out the individual needs of each space."

"Very organized."

She nodded. "That's the general idea," she said, turning away from him to return to her chair. "That's the gist of what Quality Interior Design does."

"And you evidently do it very well. John said you came highly recommended, and he is extremely pleased with the results."

"Most of our clients are." Setting her coffee down, she added, "We save them money, time, and inconvenience. And frustration when they have trouble finding something. You experienced that when you wanted to find your dartboard and drinks dispenser."

"Both are still missing," he reminded her.

"If you had taken the time to read the instructions left in your desk, you would have discovered they weren't— What was the word you used earlier?"

He grinned. "Nicked."

Coral smiled. "Your valuable office equipment wasn't nicked after all, Mr. Forge." She leaned over to press a couple of keys on the computer. Studying the information displayed on the screen, she said, "The two bottom drawers of the file cabinet closest to the window are false. Inside you will find a small refrigerator fully stocked with your usual brand of soft drink. The dartboard is behind the print of four men in clown costumes and makeup sitting around a table playing poker or some other sort of game that requires a considerable amount of chips, cigars, and beer. As you can see, we didn't replace your artwork. We try to incorporate as many personal touches as possible so that the clients feel comfortable with their own things around them. I remember seeing your painting. It's an interesting choice of subject. Is there any particular significance I've missed about clowns playing cards, or is it a male thing I wouldn't be able to grasp?"

Paul sipped his coffee, then said, "Any game involving gambling should be played for fun whether it's cards, climbing a mountain, taking a trip down whitewater rapids in a kayak, or dealing with a woman. Each has a certain amount of risk."

"You have an odd idea of fun, Mr. Forge."

"Maybe," he conceded. He tilted his head to one side to study her face from a different angle. "What do you do for fun, Miss Bentley?"

"What makes you think I'm not enjoying myself right now?"

"Even if you like your work, it's still your job. What happens to Coral Bentley when she walks out of the doors of Quality Interior Design at the end of the day?"

"Not a lot," she admitted, slightly abashed to realize what she said was all too true. "I hope you aren't going to bring out that old straw about all work and no play will make Coral a dull girl."

"I wouldn't think of it," he said. "Even if I thought it was true. My mother raised me to be a gentleman no matter what the circumstances. I was just thinking that since your company has done such a valuable service for Outfitters, we could reciprocate by offering to set up a holiday for you."

"You came in here ranting and raving about the condition of your office, demanding that I have everything put back the way it was. Now all of a sudden we've done a terrific job?"

"I did not rant and rave," he said with a hint of indignation. "And I'm not trying to bribe you. I don't expect you to do something for nothing. You arrange to have my office put back to normal, and I'll set up a special holiday for you in return."

She shook her head, amused by his assumption that she wouldn't be able to turn down such an offer. "I don't think so. I'm a good sport only when it comes to losing at card games and waiting in long lines at the bank and the grocery store. I've never had the time nor the inclination to get into competitive sports."

"I don't think you understand the type of holidays we arrange. We don't assign people to play on professional football teams. They go whitewater rafting or skiing or fishing or climb mountains, a number of activities that don't involve competing against anyone."

"They compete against nature or themselves. As much as I appreciate your offer, I'll pass. I have a healthy respect for my body and prefer to keep it all in one piece. Thank you."

"That's unfortunate." He paused, then said thoughtfully, "It's not going to work out between us, after all, is it? And I had such plans for us. You would want to take the children to the seashore, and I'd want the family with me when I went on safari in East Africa."

"Darn," she said with a smile. "I'll have to take back the wallpaper samples I picked out for the nursery."

Paul chuckled. At that moment the door of Coral's office swung open, and Louise entered. She wheeled up to Coral's desk and handed Coral the plump file she'd had on her lap.

"Will it be necessary for me to call Midvale and cancel your appointment?" she asked.

Coral glanced at the slim watch on her wrist. "I'll only be another ten minutes or so with Mr. Forge, Louise. There's no need to cancel Midvale. Or," she murmured as she opened the file, "to summon Security. I've been reassured by Mr. Forge that his mother brought him up to be a perfect gentleman, so you see, we have nothing to worry about. He was just a tiny bit upset that we had moved a few things around in his office without permission."

Louise sent a puzzled frown in Paul's direction. "We had permission." Looking at Coral, she added, "I typed the contract myself, and Mr. Keats signed it."

"We didn't have Mr. Forge's consent to invade his personal space." Coral met Paul's gaze. "I have a suggestion to make in order to settle your complaint."

He gave her a wary look. "And what is your suggestion?"

"Try the new system for two weeks." She held up her hand when he started to speak. "If by the end of that time, you find you can't live with the more convenient, organized way of doing business, then I'll attempt to put your office back the way it was. A stick of dynamite or a powerful fan directed on your files should about do it."

Paul grinned. She had a way of putting her

claws in without cutting too deeply, yet the digs were there. A few minutes ago he would have said he wouldn't accept anything short of his office being put back exactly the way it had been. Now he was actually considering the trial run she'd offered.

"On one condition," he stated.

Coral's eyes widened in surprise. She hadn't expected him to go for her suggestion. "What is the condition?"

"If I have any problems locating something, you will help me find it."

She gave his request a brief consideration. It really wasn't that much to ask. Her staff had occasionally returned to a client's home or business to demonstrate and explain the changes they had made. As a compromise it was fairly painless.

"All right, I agree." She turned to Louise. "If Mr. Forge phones with a problem, forward the request to Steven or Edie."

Both women looked at Paul when he said, "No."

Coral sighed heavily. "What's wrong now?"

"Not Steve and Edie," he said.

"Steven, not Steve. You're thinking of the singers."

"What singers?"

Their merry-go-round conversation had revolved one too many turns, and she was getting dizzy. "Never mind. Steven and Edie are familiar with the work that was done at Outfitters. As I told you earlier, I did the initial survey and planned the changes, but the staff who actually did the job can be of more help to you than I can."

He shook his head. "You take my phone calls or no deal."

Feeling pressured, Coral ignored Louise's finger tapping on the face of her watch, indicating Coral was running out of time. She stared at Paul Forge. His gaze was level, one corner of his mouth turned upward in a hint of a smile.

He was issuing a challenge, and she could either accept it or possibly lose a customer.

Unable to surrender totally, she said, "If I can spare the time, I'll try to help you adjust to the new system. If, on the other hand, I feel you need more specialized instruction, I'll send over one of my staff who worked on the installation."

"You," he repeated.

Louise made a choking sound as though she had physically swallowed whatever it was she wanted to say. Coral knew the feeling. A few choice words had come to her mind too. Such as *arrogant*, *pushy*, and *stubborn*.

She pushed her chair back and stood. "We'll see. Right now I have a meeting scheduled with a client, so if you'll excuse me, Mr. Forge, I'd like to keep my appointment."

Paul placed his hands on the arms of his chair and got to his feet. This time he didn't try to get in the last word. He was quite satisfied with the results of his meeting, even if they weren't what he'd expected when he'd stormed into Coral's office.

As he left, he suppressed the urge to grin in triumph, settling for a more dignified exit. When he stood in front of the elevator, though, he couldn't help laughing aloud, unconcerned that he'd startled the older man walking past him.

TWO

The first distress call from Paul came the following morning. Without any preliminaries or pleasantries he announced, "Your staff has really screwed up this time."

Coral swiveled her chair around so that she could look out the window.

"Mr. Forge, I presume?"

"Damn straight. Who trained your staff? The Marx brothers?"

"What did the little mischief makers do now?"

"Don't try that martyred tone with me. I'm on to you. This is serious."

"My humble apologies." She was beginning to enjoy herself. "I was only trying to find out the severity of your complaint so that I can determine the appropriate punishment for their crime."

With renewed indignation he said, "They didn't make a file for the post."

"Why would you want a file for a post to begin with?"

"Not *a* post. *The* post. Letters, correspondence. Envelopes with stamps on them shoved into letterboxes by postmen carrying heavy satchels."

"Ah, well, that's because you have an American filing system. What you call post my staff thinks of as the mail."

"I figured that out, Miss Bentley. I didn't just come to the States without a book of translations. I couldn't find a file with that heading either."

"That's because your letters would have been put into a file marked 'Correspondence.'"

After a short pause Paul said, "Let's see if I have this right. A letter that comes through the mail, which is actually the post, would be in a folder marked 'Correspondence.'"

The dry note in his voice made Coral smile. "By Jove, I think he's got it!"

"I don't know why I'm having trouble finding anything, Miss Doolittle. It's all so terribly clear."

Coral was smiling when he hung up the phone.

At the other end of the line Paul frowned as he replaced the receiver. He couldn't remember the last time he'd wanted to talk to a woman on the phone just so that he could hear her voice. Even as a teenager with raging hormones, he hadn't lingered on the phone, preferring action to words. Leaning back in his chair, he realized he wouldn't mind something more personal with Coral Bentley.

He had no idea of the exact moment when his assessment of her changed from average to alluring. Maybe it had been when she'd crossed her office to her coffeepot and he'd seen that her legs were as long and as shapely as a runway model's. Or maybe it had been when they'd been teasing each other about the children they wouldn't have, when the mischievous light in her eyes and her smile gave her whole face an unexpected beauty. Whenever it had happened, his feelings toward her had altered. He didn't understand why, any more than he could explain why he was eager to find out how her mouth would feel under his or how he would react to having her body pressed against his.

One of these days he was going to satisfy his curiosity.

That was Tuesday. He phoned twice on Wednesday with similar problems, lingering on the line after she'd given him an explanation regarding his inquiry. Coral didn't mind the interruptions as much as she'd thought she would. She was always smiling when their conversations ended, and she realized by Friday morning as she entered her office that she was actually look-ing forward to Paul's next call.

She didn't have to wait long.

She smiled in anticipation as Louise an-nounced it, then she frowned. She needed to get a life, she decided. If the highlight of her day was hearing Paul Forge's cultured tones berating her company's organizational methods, then she had better seriously rearrange her priorities.

She picked up the phone and, using her best professional voice, said, "What seems to be the problem today, Mr. Forge?"

"You calling me Mr. Forge, for starters," he answered. "Any woman who knows the intimate details of a man's filing system should be on a first-name basis with him at least."

Since she'd used his first name off and on during the last few days, it was an easy conces-sion to make. "All right, Paul. Do you have a reason for calling other than straightening out the first-versus-last-name question?"

His deep chuckle traveled through the phone line. "You have such a smart mouth, Coral. I never thought I would be susceptible to a woman with claws, even if they are wrapped in velvet."

Coral glanced at her fingernails. They were medium length, polished with a clear coat as usual, and she wondered what in heck he was talking about. "You, on the other hand, have a habit of pouncing on any subject other than the one you started out with."

"I do?"

"You do. Did you have a specific question about your poor, mistreated office?"

"Probably, or else I was just calling to hear your charming voice." He paused. "What was it I was going to ask you? I've forgotten."

"How would I know why you called?" It wasn't all that easy to talk through gritted teeth. "You immediately started in about me using your first name."

"I remember now." In his office Paul propped a foot on top of his desk and picked up a paper clip and a rubber band. Tucking the phone in the crook of his shoulder, he released the stretched rubber band and watched the paper clip sail across the room, barely missing the lampshade that was his target. "A friend of my brother's wants to do some fly-fishing, and I can't find the brochure on the lodge in Scotland I was going to recommend. It was on the right-hand corner of my desk before I left, and now it's gone."

"Did you think to look in the files?" she asked patiently.

"I'm not a complete moron, Coral. I sorted through all those lovely colorful tabs under 'Brochures,' 'Trout,' 'Scotland,' and 'Fly-fishing.' Nothing. It's not here."

"Try looking under 'Fishing,'" she suggested.

"I just told you I looked under 'Fly-fishing.'"

"I heard you. Try 'Fishing' without the *fly*."

"If I were interested in fishing without a fly, I wouldn't want information on fly-fishing in the first place, now, would I?"

"Do you want my help or not?"

"All right," he muttered as he pushed back his chair. "There's no need to get testy. I'll look in the files."

Coral smiled at the grudging tone in his voice. "Take me with you."

The muted sounds of Paul's movement ceased abruptly, as though someone had pulled a switch. She couldn't even hear him breathing.

"Paul?" she said. She clicked the connection button twice, then called his name again. "Paul?"

"Still here."

"I thought we'd been disconnected."

"Someone just cut into the line and said, 'Take me with you.'"

"That was me."

"Where exactly did you want me to take you?"

"To the filing cabinet."

"What a disappointment," he murmured. Paul stepped over to the cabinet, tucking the phone receiver between his jaw and shoulder, and pulled open the top drawer. He riffled through the folders. "Did you know there's about a hundred files here that begin with the word *Fishing*?"

"Try looking under 'Fishing-dash-fly,'" Coral said.

"I need information on fly-dash-fishing, not fishing while flying."

"Humor me."

Paul found the file she mentioned. "'Fishing-fly,'" he announced with a great deal of satisfaction. "Not to be confused with 'Fishing-deep-sea,' 'Fishing-fresh,' 'Fishing-saltwater,' or 'Fishing-salmon.'" Taking the file with him, he returned to his desk. Opening the folder, he found the brochure he wanted tucked inside. Sounding a little deflated, he said, "The brochure is here."

"It's not easy, but I'm refraining from saying I told you so."

"Don't go patting yourself on the back just yet. I could have given the information to Reggie when he called from England if the brochure had been where it was supposed to be."

"Is Reggie your brother or your friend who wants to go fishing?"

"My brother."

Why was she prolonging this conversation? Coral wondered. She could easily list a number of things she could be doing other than chatting with Paul Forge. Unfortunately she couldn't think of a single one that she'd rather be doing.

"Is Reggie your brother's nickname?" she asked.

"Actually his name is Reginald Malcolm Strothmore Tysdale Denton-Forge. Just Reggie for obvious reasons."

"I bet he had a lot of fun on the playground when he was in school."

"It wasn't as much of a problem as you would think. Some of his classmates were called Binky, Gaspar, and I believe there was an Ospert, who had a cousin named Aloysius. Reginald was fairly tame stuff."

"You're making that up," she said, smiling.

"Not entirely. Part of the reason Reggie didn't have any difficulties with the bully-boys was due to his being a scrappy lad big for his age. One of his mates from school is the bloke who wants to go fly-fishing."

"And you would have been able to provide the information if the brochure had been on the corner of your desk along with a foot-high stack of other papers. I know. I heard you the first time."

"My way might not have been up to your standards, but I knew where everything was. I thought this new system was supposed to save time."

"It will once you get used to it."

"I'm not sure I can become accustomed to thinking Fishing-dash-fly when I mean Fly-dash-fishing."

"Think of the overall subject first—like golf, for example. Then break it down into categories. Domestic, international, tournaments—that sort of thing."

"I must be filing-dash-impaired," he said with an exaggerated sigh.

She smiled. "Give yourself time."

"Which reminds me," he said quickly. "It's almost time for lunch. Why don't I come by for you and, over a bowl of soup, you can regale me with more fascinating facts about filing? If I treat you to dessert, you might even find it in your heart to explain how to use the fax machine that has mysteriously appeared on the credenza."

"Sorry," she said automatically, then realized she actually was. "I don't have time for lunch today. I have exactly twenty minutes to get to my next appointment. If you have any problems this afternoon, you will have to talk to Louise."

"Your secretary will undoubtedly instruct me on where I can go and how fast I should get there." He gave a martyred sigh. "I'll bungle along the best I can on my own."

"How brave of you," she said. She looked up as her door opened and Louise entered the office. "I really must go. You might find this hard to believe, but we actually have other clients besides Outfitters."

"Hopefully none of them is going to monopolize your time as much as I am. One of these

days I'm not going to take no for an answer."
His voice grew a bit deeper, his accent even
more pronounced and charming. "You know
that, don't you? And it's going to be soon."

Coral fidgeted with a pen. She tried to keep
her own voice sounding professional, but she
didn't think she was very successful. "I don't recall saying no to any of your questions."

"I'm not talking about business. I want to see
you again, if not for lunch, then some other time
when you aren't thinking about appointments or
anything else but me. Go do what you've got to
do, Coral. I'll talk to you later."

Coral frowned as the line went dead in her
ear. She wasn't sure whether his comment had
been a threat or a promise. Possibly both, she
thought. She wasn't surprised that he had suggested seeing her away from the office. She had
been aware of the underlying attraction growing
between them during their bantering conversations. What did surprise her was the strength of
her own desire to know Paul Forge better.

As Louise stopped her chair on the other
side of the desk, Coral glanced at the phone
she'd just hung up. "Mr. Forge of Outfitters
might be calling you this afternoon if he has any
other problems finding something."

"The only problem that man has is he is too
accustomed to getting his own way. You can tell
by his manner. He's not weak in the pushy department."

Coral picked up her pen to sign the letters her secretary placed in front of her. "Some people might say the same thing about me. A certain amount of aggression is necessary in order to run a business. You saw the size of the offices and the number of people employed at Outfitters. They are apparently very successful. John Keats gave Paul Forge equal credit for the growth of the company."

"When I said he was accustomed to getting his own way," Louise said, "I wasn't just referring to business. He isn't shy about wanting you at his beck and call."

Coral handed the signed letters back. "*Shy* isn't one of the words I would use to describe Paul Forge in any category."

"I could give his calls to the barracuda instead of putting them through to you. She would either wear him out or turn him off. Either way you wouldn't have to bother with him."

"One of these days Marie is going to hear you refer to her as a barracuda and aim some of her renowned Spanish temperament in your direction."

"She probably wouldn't mind." Louise grinned. "She enjoys her reputation for having the most dates a month. It's a shame she's so darn nice. It would give me such pleasure to dislike her for her success with the opposite sex." Louise grimaced as she glanced down at her small chest. "Of course if I had the kind of bait she has, I could probably land one or two myself."

"Did you have fish for lunch?"

Louise blinked. "No. Why?"

"I was curious where all the fish metaphors were coming from."

Tilting her head to one side, Louise considered the subject. "He reminds me of a shark. Paul Forge," she added when Coral gave her a blank look. "He's quick, sharp, and attacks without any warning, like the other day when he barged into your office. My impression of him was he could be very dangerous to any woman who thinks he would be happy in captivity."

"And what do you base this theory on?"

"Keen observation." Louise chuckled when Coral raised her eyebrows. "And a bit of gossip I picked up when I had coffee in the employees' lounge at Outfitters while Mr. Keats was giving you the grand tour."

"I'm surprised at you, Louise. My mother says that listening to gossip is for those people who have idle minds to match their idle hands."

"So do you want to hear what they said or not?"

Coral leaned forward. "Of course."

Louise grinned. "According to one of the travel agents who has worked for the company almost from the beginning, Paul Forge is one of those strange minority of people who work because they want to, not because they have to earn their daily bread."

Coral was used to Louise's penchant for drawing out a point until it was dull. "Are you saying he's rich?"

"I'm not saying it. The people at Outfitters said it. I also gathered from listening to some of their anecdotes, he put the word *play* into *playboy*. Forge scouts out potential resorts, fishing spots, and ski slopes while Keats tends to the dull stuff of making the actual arrangements for the trips and sending out the bills."

Coral couldn't help but make the comparison between Paul Forge and John Keats, and her family and herself. Behind every free spirit there was a practical person who put bread on the table and arranged for a roof over the free spirit's head. She had always been that overly responsible person. All the other members of her family relied on her to take care of the mundane matters of life, leaving them to pursue their experiments, their writing, and their inventions. They were able to live and work in their rarefied scientific worlds as long as she arranged for their food, clothing, and necessary supplies.

"A rich playboy," she mused aloud. "I didn't realize there were all that many of the breed left."

"Sure there are," said Louise. "They've just changed their title. Around here they call themselves politicians."

Coral laughed. "Either way, playboy or politician, Paul Forge is way out of my league."

Louise turned her chair toward the door. "You just keep telling yourself that when he phones again."

"The reason he keeps calling is because he's trying to adjust to an office where he can actually see the top of his desk." When Louise threw her a skeptical look over her shoulder, Coral added, "All right. And to give me a hard time for the fun of it."

"You never can tell with men," Louise said. "He might just be serious about pestering you on a long-term basis."

"It'll be a cold day in hell before Paul Forge is serious about anything."

Hell froze over about four o'clock the following afternoon.

Coral had just returned to the office after a hectic morning of meetings and an afternoon appointment with a couple who wanted their new business set up to their own exact and peculiar standards before they opened their doors to the public.

Coral's arm was straight and stiff like a knight aiming a lance as she pushed open the glass door to Quality Interior's outer office. Her briefcase slammed against her thigh as she marched across the carpet toward Louise's desk.

"Do I look like a complete nincompoop, Louise?"

Her secretary gave Coral a thorough examination over the top of her glasses. "Not completely. Why?"

"Mr. and Mrs. Fogarty of Fogarty's Bait and Tackle want Quality Interiors to design more efficient and at the same time more attractive holding tanks for the live bait they will be selling. Correct me if I'm wrong, but aren't the minnows, worms, and other creepy-crawling things they sell supposed to be yummy to fish, not people?"

"Is that a trick question?"

Coral plopped down in the chair closest to Louise's desk. "It's a stupid question. Just as dumb as the Fogartys' request for a layered tank that would hold more fish. How can I design something to attract fishermen into buying bait that they wouldn't eat if they were starving? If the fish marched in and bought the stuff, I might have something to work with."

"So what did you tell the Fogartys?"

"I suggested they contact the Smithsonian, Marineworld, and an advertising agency. Our company can improvise and organize, but not fantasize. We've taken on a few clients who didn't fit the normal customer profile, but I draw the line at fish."

"I'll make a note of that."

Coral slowly got to her feet. "I hope that's

the last appointment for the day. I feel the need for a soothing cup of herbal tea and ten minutes of feeling sorry for myself."

At that moment the phone on Louise's desk trilled.

"It's probably your favorite sportsman," she told Coral. "Forge has phoned twice in the last hour."

As Coral rolled her eyes, Louise answered the phone.

"Ah, Mr. Forge," she said, grinning. "How nice to hear from you again. How may I help you?"

Coral shook her head violently and tiptoed in an exaggerated fashion toward the door of her office.

In the doorway she stopped to look back at Louise when her secretary didn't say anything more to Paul. Coral was completely baffled by the expression on Louise's face as she listened to Paul. If she didn't know Louise's opinion of Paul Forge, Coral would have guessed her secretary was genuinely concerned.

Finally Louise said, "Miss Bentley just came in, Mr. Forge. I'm sure she'll be able to help you."

Coral waited until Louise had put the call on hold. "If I had the strength, I'd fire you. Why did you tell him I was here?"

"You can't fire me. I have the only key to the rest room, and I know where the coffee is hidden." Becoming serious, she returned to Paul's phone call. "I think you should talk to him. He sounds really distracted about something. He said it was a matter of life and death."

"Which means he probably forgot how to operate his new electric pencil sharpener," Coral said in a dry tone.

As she walked into her office, Louise called out a few words of comfort. "At least dealing with Paul Forge will be more entertaining than the last couple of hours with the Fogartys."

"So would a root canal," Coral called back.

She didn't need to see Louise to know she was shuddering at the reminder of the dental procedure she'd endured the previous week.

Coral pulled the phone across her desk, tucking the receiver in the crook of her neck while she shrugged out of her suit jacket.

"Hello, Paul. What have you lost today?"

"My mind," he said curtly.

"Tell us something we don't know." She could have sworn she heard him gnashing his teeth, and smiled. "I'll rephrase the question. What can I do for you today?"

"You can get over here as fast as you can. Faster if possible. I'll pay any speeding tickets you might get. Just trot yourself over to my office unless you want my death on your hands."

"Death? That's a little dramatic, isn't it, Paul? Even for you?"

"You don't know my sister." He lowered his

voice. "Hurry, she'll be here any minute." Then he hung up.

Whether it was the urgency in his voice or just plain curiosity, Coral slipped her jacket back on and grabbed her purse. Oddly enough, the exhaustion she'd been feeling a minute earlier had magically disappeared, replaced by anticipation humming through her entire body.

Shutting her office door behind her, she walked over to Louise. "I'll be at Outfitters if you need me for anything before"—she looked at her watch—"before the end of the workday, which is exactly twelve minutes from now. Never mind. I have a better idea. Let's live dangerously and both leave twelve minutes early. The answering service can take our calls."

Louise needed no extra persuasion. She turned off her computer and cleared off the top of her desk with lightning efficiency. Before she had called the answering service, though, the phone on her desk rang. She was unable to ignore the call.

As Louise answered the phone, Coral checked to see that she had everything she needed in her purse and briefcase. She barely paid attention to what she was doing, though. Most of her thoughts were on Paul Forge and whatever awaited her at Outfitters. Usually after a day full of problems she wasn't in the mood to take on any more, but she realized she was looking forward to the meeting with Paul.

At the moment she didn't feel it was necessary to examine or analyze her motives very deeply. Sparring with Paul Forge was fun. She felt a strange energy reverberate along her nerve endings whenever she talked to him. She likened it to the crisp, rapid popping of bubbles in a glass of champagne.

Louise waved her hand in a sweeping motion to get Coral's attention, and held the phone out to her when she finally had it. "It's your father."

Coral didn't hesitate to take the call. No matter what she was doing or who she was with at the time, she had instructed Louise that her family had priority over anyone or anything else.

Rather than return to her office to take the call, she took the receiver from Louise and leaned her hip against her secretary's desk. Since her father did not like talking on the telephone at any time, Coral was concerned that he was phoning this late in the day when he knew she would be arriving at Fields of Honey that evening as usual for the weekend.

"Hi, Pop. Did you think of something else you want me to bring with me?"

Dennis Bentley had more than enough college degrees to paper one wall of a small room, yet he always spoke loudly into the phone as though it were a relatively recent invention and they hadn't worked all the bugs out of it yet.

Accordingly Coral held the phone several inches from her ear as her father said, "Your mother forgot to tell you she needs ten pounds of spelt flour and a dozen cans of miso soup along with the other things on her list."

"No problem. I'll pick them up on the way."

She waited for her father to get around to the real reason for the phone call. Dennis Bentley had two speeds in which he accomplished most things during his waking hours: fast and stop. He rarely coasted even in conversation. The older man could be incredibly patient with his various research projects, but when it came to people or practical matters, he became impatient with normal conversation and the mundane details it took to get through a day.

Finally he said, "This morning, your brother reminded me about your mother's birthday. Guthrie said it's a week from Sunday."

"That's right." Coral smiled. Her father could quote complicated statistics concerning the life cycle of most arthropods, but rarely knew what day it was.

"What plans have you kids made for her party?"

"Guthrie and Harry are setting up several benches and the projection screen in her favorite glade by the creek under the large oak tree. Harry and the kids are going to string fairy lights in some of the smaller trees, and Nadine and I will provide the popcorn and cider. With the help of Guthrie's generator and Harry's video player, we plan to show her favorite movie under the stars."

"*The Sound of Music?*"

"Yes," she said, surprised he'd remembered. "We thought she'd enjoy the movie outdoors instead of inside."

"Hmmm" was the only response she received.

"Pop," she said with resigned patience. When she received no response, she tried again, "Pop!"

"What is it, Coral?" he asked brusquely as though she'd just interrupted an important thought.

"You can do musical-response tests on your bugs another time, okay? We could all do with a night off, including you. Your insect friends might appreciate it too."

He chuckled. "You know me so well. I give you my word. No experiments, even if I see a seven-legged honeybee. Am I supposed to do anything?"

"At sunset you're to suggest she go for a walk with you. She'll think it's to get her out of the house so that we can get everything ready for the surprise when you return. Instead you'll lead her to the party in the woods."

"Ah, yes. I remember now."

"Don't worry, Pop," Coral said with tolerant amusement. "You don't need to do anything else. Just escort her to the party."

"I wasn't worried. I was only surprised when Guthrie mentioned it, that's all."

Along with being exceptionally brilliant, her father was a stickler for routine. Any deviation threw him off balance. Coral and her brothers and her sister-in-law did their best to act as buffers to give the retired professor the space and time he needed for his studies and his experiments.

"Go back to your work, Pop. I'll be home in a couple of hours."

Reassured, her father said good-bye and hastily hung up.

Coral glanced at her watch. "We can close officially now," she said to Louise. "It's after five."

"Is everything all right with your family?"

Coral adjusted the strap of her purse. "My father tends to get rattled when his routine is changed. Then it's like the domino effect. He disrupts Harry, who nudges Guthrie, who bumps into Nadine, and so on. They all live so close together, it only takes one of them to affect the mood of the others." She held the main door open so that Louise could maneuver her wheelchair out into the hall. "You've seen my family enough to know how they are."

"The first time I went to Fields of Honey, your father interrupted a game of Monopoly to check something to do with pollen count. That gave me a clue your parents were not the naive country bumpkins I thought they would be."

"You think anyone who lives in the suburbs are hicks."

"I'm a city person, born and bred. I don't understand the appeal of wide-open spaces where deer and buffalo roam."

Coral chuckled. "The area around Charlottesville, Virginia, is not exactly uncharted territory."

"I admit it isn't as primitive as I thought it would be. In fact I have had a great time whenever I've gone home with you. The one thing your family isn't is boring. They live on a somewhat elevated plane of consciousness, yet by the end of the weekend I felt like I'm one of them."

"Not everyone understands their way of life, but snoopy people aren't a problem at the Fields. In the nearest town they aren't aware that a man who has won every prestigious award given by the scientific community lives in the vicinity. They won't hear about the kind of work my father does if it's up to him. He and the rest of the Bentleys at the Fields want their privacy. My family doesn't quite fit into society's neat little grooves."

"I know what that's like." Louise patted the arm of her wheelchair. "It sounds like you're going to have another busy weekend. I hope you've packed my grandmother's recipe for honey-glazed ham I promised to give to Nadine."

"I have it. I just hope the traffic will have thinned out by the time I finish at Outfitters. I still have a couple of stops to make after I see Paul Forge."

"You're going to Outfitters now?"

"It's not that far out of my way, and he did sound shaken."

"Why didn't you put Forge off until Monday?"

Coral smiled wryly. "It can't be done."

THREE

Traffic in D.C. was never a peaceful Sunday drive at the best of times, not even on a Sunday. Morning and evening rush hour during the week was more like a game of chance where everyone took a number and hoped it didn't come up during the trip.

Coral had plenty of miles of driving experience logged in all types of weather, seasons, and conditions, which was why she found it odd that she was feeling apprehensive as she took the exit that would lead her to Outfitters. Maybe it had been the hint of panic in Paul's voice. All the other times she'd talked to him, he had teased, grumbled, complained, and pouted about the changes in his office, but to be fair, he hadn't been seriously angry just because a couple of items weren't where he thought they should be.

To be angry would mean he felt strongly

about something, and Coral wasn't sure Paul was capable of feeling deeply about anyone or anything. It was only one of the doubts she had about him that kept her from seriously considering her desire to know him better.

That evening, though, his voice on the phone had contained an unusual tone she'd never heard before. After such a short acquaintance she could hardly call herself an expert on Paul Forge's moods, but she'd sensed that this time he was anxious about the lost item. The desperation in his voice struck a responsive chord deep inside her that she couldn't ignore. She had felt compelled to go to him when he asked for her.

She liked thinking he needed her.

Lord knows, being needed wasn't a revolutionary concept in her life, she rationalized. Her family depended on her calm, practical nature to keep their lives running smoothly, and she liked the feeling of contributing, of giving to the people she loved.

Which had nothing to do with her response to Paul Forge's phone call, she told herself. Tending to a client's request was good for business. It was no more complicated than that.

Fortunately Coral managed to find a parking spot fairly close to the building where the Outfitters' office was located. Parking in that area of the city was similar to looking for gold in a rockslide. Just when she thought she'd spotted one, an avalanche of other cars were there to take the valuable nugget away.

A few minutes later she entered the lobby and walked toward the bank of elevators. She only made it halfway there when someone took her arm.

"Miss Bentley?"

Startled, Coral turned her head toward the uniformed security guard who was looming over her like a solid oak tree. The sharply pressed uniform and holstered gun didn't intimidate her as much as the knowledge that his fingers easily wrapped around her upper arm.

"Yes?" she answered cautiously. "I'm Coral Bentley."

"Come with me, please," he said in a somber tone that did absolutely nothing to reassure her.

Instead of continuing on toward the elevators, the large guard drew her toward a door on the opposite side of the lobby. Coral felt as if she were a package he was going to deliver.

"Wait a minute," she protested. "Where are you taking me?"

"Take it easy, Miss Bentley. We aren't going far."

"I'll relax when you let go of my arm."

"I'm kinda in a hurry, miss. I'm not supposed to be away from my desk."

"So it's easier to drag me along with you?"

"It seems so. I'm just following orders."

"What kind of orders, Earl?" she asked,

reading his name on the small plastic tag pinned to his shirt pocket. "And who gave them to you?"

"The kind I obey when they're given by one of the suits in this building who pay my salary." Earl reached over her head and pushed the door open in front of them. "Mr. Forge asked me to escort you to the VIP suite before you go up to his office."

At the mention of Paul's name her apprehension changed to resignation. She no longer worried about being clamped in handcuffs and led away to the pokey on some trumped-up charge. She allowed herself a small smile, amused by the turn her imagination had taken. Usually it was her family who had the exclusive rights to imaginative ideas, not her.

Coral stepped through the doorway onto a plush maroon carpet with a gold border on each side that stretched along the hallway ahead of them. The guard released his hold on her arm and walked beside her, passing several closed doors without even giving them a glance.

When the silence became too oppressive, Coral said, "I'm curious about something, Earl."

"Mr. Forge will answer any of your questions, miss."

"How did you know I was the person Mr. Forge wanted? There must have been about thirty people in that lobby when I came in, and half of them were women."

Stopping in front of a closed door, Earl smiled at her. "Mr. Forge said I was to detain a lady with short brown hair and of average height who would look like the girl next door, until I saw her drop-dead gorgeous brown eyes that were the color of sinfully rich dark chocolate." His gaze took in the tapestry-print vest she wore under a white jacket and with a green skirt. "He also said she was one of those rare ladies who can dress like a man and still look like a woman."

Coral's reaction vacillated between indignation and pleasure at Paul's backhanded compliment. She was relieved that Earl had turned to open the door and didn't seem to expect a comment from her. She couldn't think of a single thing to say.

At least not to Earl.

Following Earl, she walked into an elegantly furnished room. An oriental rug in shades of wine, dark green, gold, and white took up the vast expanse of carpet not covered by plush couches and upholstered chairs. Gilt-and-glass-trimmed tables with large fresh floral arrangements in fat raku vases competed with several mahogany Queen Anne desks that supported impressive arrays of telephones, fax machines, and pristine pads of paper positioned near them for those all-important notes.

The room was also quite empty.

"I can think of worse places to be held captive," she murmured.

"Would you like some coffee, Miss Bentley? Or perhaps a soda or juice while you wait for Mr. Forge?"

"No, thanks anyway, Earl." Coral turned to the security guard. "If this is your idea of kidnapping me for ransom, you're going to be seriously disappointed. My father could probably round up a couple of jars of honey for you and several copies of some of the books he's written, but those are about the only tangible assets he has. My older brother is the strong, silent type, more comfortable with plants than with people. He could possibly bring you some vegetables out of his garden, but I wouldn't count on any cold cash if I were you. My other brother designs, builds, and fixes clocks but rarely knows what time it is. You've grabbed the wrong potential money maker, Earl. You make more in a week than I'd be able to get you from my family."

A corner of Earl's mouth curved up in amusement. "I haven't kidnapped you, Miss Bentley. As I told you earlier, Mr. Forge asked me to bring you here for your meeting."

"So where is he? He made it sound as though it was a life-or-death matter and that I had to get over here as soon as I could, yet he doesn't appear to be waiting for me."

"I don't know, miss. The last time I saw Mr. Forge, he was hiding in the men's rest room from his sister. That's when he asked me to corral you when you arrived and bring you here."

"Thank you so much, Earl," Paul said from behind them, closing a door on the other side of the room. "Every man wants his women friends to think he's a raging coward. I wasn't hiding from Lindsay. I was simply choosing the right time to confront her."

Coral watched Paul as he walked toward her. He looked long and lean and lazy in gray slacks and a white shirt with a patterned gray tie. If Paul was nervous about seeing his sister or felt any guilt at the treatment Coral had received from the security guard, he was very good at hiding either emotion.

He stopped beside her and slipped his left arm around her waist in a casual, yet possessive gesture she was totally unprepared for. Anyone seeing the easy intimacy of his greeting would assume they were more than acquaintances. She could tell Earl had put that interpretation on Paul's actions by the knowing look he was bestowing on them.

She couldn't really blame Earl for coming to that conclusion. For a few seconds when she'd felt Paul's arm wrap around her, she had thought his touch was perfectly natural, the way it should be between them.

Then reality set in, and she wondered what game Paul was playing. Still, she didn't move away from him.

Holding his right hand out to the security guard, Paul said, "Thanks, Earl. I really appreciate this."

"No problem," the other man replied as he briefly shook Paul's hand. "Glad I could be of some assistance. I was young once myself, you know."

"I don't doubt it for a minute. How about some refreshments before you return to your desk?"

"Thanks, Mr. Forge, but I'd better get back."

The guard's manner changed suddenly, dramatically, and self-consciously. He bit his bottom lip and a faint pink color rose in his cheeks. Coral expected to see him shuffle his feet any minute.

"Anything you need, you have only to ask, Mr. Forge," Earl said. "Edna and I'll never be able to repay you for helping Jay get into that school in London. We'd never have been able to manage if you hadn't helped us with the scholarship and the arrangements."

Paul dismissed the man's gratitude with a wave of his hand. "All I did was put you in touch with a couple of people. Your son has a lot of talent. It would be a shame if he wasn't able to do anything with it."

Coral was aware, even if Earl wasn't, that while they were talking, Paul was easing toward the door she and the guard had used a few minutes ago.

"Thanks again for your help, Earl," he said as he opened the door. "I think I can handle things from here."

To Coral's amazement the taciturn guard actually winked at her, said "Miss," and left the room.

After the door was closed, Coral turned to Paul. "You did a nice thing."

He smiled at the touch of reproach in her voice. "You make it sound as though I'm guilty of just the opposite. All I did was have Earl escort you in here rather than meet you in my office. Is that so terrible?"

"I mean about helping his son get into a school in London."

"I made a few phone calls. That's all. He's an extremely gifted lad who needed a break, and I happened to know some people who could give him one."

"Why did you have to do something sweet and generous like that?" she said irritably. "Now I have to readjust my opinion of you, and I was enjoying thinking you were a spoiled playboy who only thought of himself."

His smile deepening, Paul trailed the back of his finger over the soft skin of her cheek. "Give me a minute and I'll do or say something totally reprehensible that will put me back in your bad graces."

Coral frowned and bit her lip. "I really don't want to find anything to like about you, you know."

"I know," he said gently. "But sometimes we don't have any control over these things."

"And that doesn't bother you, does it? You prefer to just let things happen rather than try to move them in the direction you want them to go."

"I know I can't control everything in this world," he said slowly, apparently puzzled by her serious tone. "I wouldn't want to even if I could."

"We have absolutely nothing in common," she insisted. "We approach life from two opposite directions. We don't want the same things."

"Are you so sure about that?" he asked, his gaze going to her mouth.

He brushed his thumb across the small indention her teeth had made in her bottom lip. She didn't look away from his steady gaze when she felt a shiver of reaction vibrate through her.

He smiled again. "You were saying something about not wanting the same thing. Right now I want to see if you taste as exciting as I think you will, and you're curious to know what it would be like if I kissed you."

"But you aren't going to kiss me now," she said with certainty.

"I'm not?" he asked, tilting his head to one

side in order to contemplate her expression. "What would stop me?"

"Time."

He blinked, clearly confused by her answer. "What about time?"

"I think once you decide to do something, you would want to take your time doing it."

Paul closed his fingers over her shoulders and held her in front of him. "A very long time," he murmured. "Long and deep and hard, and I'm not going to wait much longer."

Coral's breath hitched in her throat at the sensual pictures his words conjured up in her mind. "Haven't you heard a word I said? We can't become involved except in business."

"Rubbish," he said as he lowered his head. Brushing his mouth over hers, he added, "I'm making it my business to become very involved with you."

Grasping for the first thing that came to mind that might stop him from kissing her again, and stop her from kissing him back, she asked, "Is this going to happen before or after your sister finds you?"

Paul moaned. Resting his forehead on hers, he muttered, "I forgot about her."

Even though she was still standing very close to him, Coral felt the easing of the sensual tension between them and relaxed a little. "Have you also forgotten the reason you asked me to come here? I doubt if it was so that we could discuss if you plan to kiss me."

"When," he said firmly.

"If," she countered.

Paul let his gaze linger on her mouth for a few more seconds, then, with a soulful sigh, trailed his hand down her arm and closed his fingers around hers.

"The fact that I could forget my sister gives you some idea of the effect you have on me," he said. "Lindsay is not an easy person to forget."

For the second time that day Coral found herself being led around like a pony with no sense of direction. Paul started walking toward the door opposite the one she'd used, and with his strong fingers wrapped around her hand she was going along whether she wanted to or not.

The door opened onto a landing between two sets of concrete-and-iron stairs, one leading upward, the other evidently going down to the basement level. When Paul headed toward the steps going up, Coral used her brilliant deductive powers to determine they were going to his office by way of the stairs.

"Is something wrong with the elevators?" she asked as she started climbing the stairs beside him.

"I don't want to take the chance of running into Lindsay on her way to the ninth floor. I'm hoping you can find what I need before she returns to my office."

"What am I supposed to be looking for?"

They had reached the second-floor landing, but Paul didn't break stride as he continued climbing. "Concert tickets."

"Excuse me?"

"Tickets to a concert. You've surely heard of such a thing. Music, singing, violins, a conductor waving a baton as though shooing away a fly. Monty's agent sent the tickets to me about two months ago, but I can't find them. Your merry munchkins have tidied them away somewhere, but I'll be damned if I can tell where."

"This is where I come in, I take it." She was beginning to feel the effects of the uphill trek, and paused to catch her breath on the fourth landing. "What happens if I can't magically produce these tickets you need so desperately?"

"I'll hear about it for the rest of my life. And not just from Lindsay. Her husband, Taylor, will grind me into the dust, as will Monty when he discovers we're not sitting in the seats he arranged for us."

A light bulb suddenly flashed in her brain, illuminating a brilliant conclusion. "Are you talking about Montego Qui, the Spanish guitarist?" Coral didn't bother trying to hide the awe in her voice. She had been unable to buy tickets for the last three concerts he'd given in D.C. "His concert on Saturday night was sold out the first day the tickets went on sale. I know because I tried to get tickets."

"The one and the same. Even if his concert wasn't sold out, I wouldn't have been able to get front-row tickets like the ones he sent for us to use. Now you can see why you have to find those tickets."

One more set of stairs to go, Coral thought thankfully when she read the number eight printed on the wall near the door. Her breathing was becoming painfully labored as she trudged on.

To keep her mind off the embarrassing effect the climb was having on her, she said, "I'm having a hard time believing you're afraid of your sister. You hike up tall, dangerous mountains and ride rapids in a flimsy rubber raft as naturally as breathing. Facing your sister without concert tickets in your hand has to be a piece of cake compared with some of the sports you indulge in. There has to be another reason you don't want to upset your sister."

"There is," Paul murmured as he paused at the landing for the ninth floor. "Lindsay is expecting a baby. She had a miscarriage last year, and it nearly killed her to lose the baby. She's been counting on seeing Monty for months, and I don't want to disappoint her."

Coral groaned audibly. And it was only partly because she could feel the beginning of a cramp in her left calf. "Dammit, Paul. You're doing it again."

He lifted his hands to show his palms. "I'm not doing anything."

"Yes, you are," she said irritably. "You're being really sweet and loving to your sister by trying to protect her from being hurt and angry in her condition."

"I'm such a cad," he admitted with a wide smile, enjoying her mock indignation. "If I were you, I would run away as fast as you can before I do something totally unforgivable, like being nice to you."

"I would if I could." She bent down to rub the offending muscle, wishing at the same time she could rid herself of the growing attraction she was feeling toward Paul. "I'll be lucky if I can even walk."

"What's wrong?" he asked innocently.

"If you'd just walked up nine flights of stairs in high-heeled shoes, you wouldn't need to ask that question."

"Sorry," he said, smiling faintly.

He knelt on one knee at her feet and moved her hands aside so that he could massage her leg.

When she tried to bat his hands away, he said, "I've had a few experiences with cramped muscles. Let me help."

Coral closed her eyes and leaned back against the wall as Paul's hands worked their magic on the taut calf muscle. She sighed with relief as the pain lessened.

"Better?"

Her response was a purr of pleasure, but Paul didn't remove his hands.

She opened her eyes when she felt his touch change, becoming a caress as his fingers slid upward past her knee. Looking down, she met his eyes and felt herself melting under the heat radiating from his gaze and the touch of his hands.

When Paul discovered she wore thigh-high stockings instead of panty hose, his fingers lingered on the bare skin between the top band and her panties. Without removing his hand, he straightened, causing her skirt to bunch up. His other hand spread over her hip, urging her against him.

When he spoke, his voice was husky, his accent more obvious than ever. "Do you know how close I am to losing my mind thinking about how good we would be together?"

Coral needed something solid to hold on to, considering her knees had become as weak as water. She placed her hands at his waist and leaned forward to bury her face in the warm curve of his neck.

"Your mother taught you to be a gentleman, remember?"

"What in bloody hell do you think is preventing me from tearing off your clothes and taking you right here and now?" he growled.

She raised her head and met his burning gaze. "My mother warned me about letting strange men touch me intimately. You are definitely strange, and certainly touching me in what I would consider an intimate area. I should be slapping your face and yelling for Earl."

"Coral?"

"Hmmm?"

"Shut up."

Her gaze remained on his mouth as he lowered his head. Then she closed her eyes and parted her lips as he claimed them. She didn't feel the cool surface of the wall at her back or hear the sounds of normal activity in the hallway on the other side of the door. All she was aware of was the weight of his body against hers, the delicious warmth of his mouth, and the excitement curling deep within her.

Breathing became secondary to feeling. And she was feeling so much, too much—all sensations of explosive pleasure. She became aware of an aching emptiness low in her body, even as a growing surge of sensual arousal filled her. The contradiction made her want to strain against him, the source of her torment and the anecdote.

Paul broke away from her mouth and buried his face in the hollow of her neck. Her scent filled his head and blurred his senses, the sound of her ragged breathing blending with his own.

His control was like a rope bridge he'd once crossed over a deep gorge, frayed to the breaking point and due to snap any second and plunge him into oblivion. The satisfaction of crossing the bridge would be exciting, but the fall if he made an error in judgment might be the worst he'd ever experienced.

He'd always trusted his instincts, and they were screaming at him that this woman was different, possibly even dangerous to his freedom. He never went into any adventure without planning every move carefully, having an escape route available in case it was needed. That had always applied to his relationships with women as well.

The realization that he was entering unknown territory with Coral should have had him looking for a safety zone, a way out of a tricky situation. But he might have waited too long to save himself, which revealed how deeply involved he was with Coral already.

Coral stroked his back, inadvertently soothing herself in the process. She could feel the tautness of the muscles under her hands and marveled in the knowledge that she had been the cause of his tension.

When he finally lifted his head and looked into her eyes, she was ready to face him. "I feel a strong desire to phone your mother," she said, "and tell her to take back her instructions on being a gentleman."

"I'll call her myself," he said roughly. He took her hand and stepped toward the door. "Let's take on my sister first."

FOUR

To Paul's chagrin Coral found the tickets in his files in two minutes flat. He had put forth an enormous effort to find them on his own. Before he'd called her as a last resort, he had gone through the entire system, compartment by compartment, file by file regardless of its heading, coming away with several paper cuts but not the envelope he needed.

He couldn't understand it. He could kayak down the most treacherous rapids in the world and sky-dive out of planes, but he couldn't conquer the mysterious workings of a simple filing system. It was humiliating.

Coral waved the white envelope with "Montego Qui Tickets" scrawled across it in front of his face, a triumphant glint in her eyes. She grinned when he snatched it out of her hand. Opening it, he took out four narrow strips of heavy paper and saw for himself that they were the tickets he wanted.

"You're welcome," she said sweetly.

"Thank you," he said with a wry smile. The door of his office opened at that moment, and he saw his sister standing in the doorway. "And none too soon," he muttered to Coral. Raising his voice, he said, "Where have you been, Lindsay? I've been looking all over for you."

"You know perfectly well you've been dodging me from the moment I entered the front office, you rat," his sister said, smiling at Paul as he walked toward her. "If you have misplaced the tickets for Monty's concert, just say so, and Taylor and I will calmly kill you and put you out of your misery."

"You must have more faith in your fellow human beings, Lindsay," Paul said as he held up the envelope containing the tickets. "I have them right here."

"Finally found them, did you?" she said as she lifted her cheek to be kissed.

As the two greeted each other, Coral studied Paul's sister with interest. The Englishwoman was much shorter than her brother; Paul had to bend his head some distance in order to kiss her. The family resemblance was there if someone looked for it, although Lindsay's features were more delicate, her frame almost too slender in the dark-green print dress she wore. Paul had said his sister was expecting, but as yet she wasn't showing her pregnancy.

Coral could easily understand Paul's concern for his sister. The other woman's frail appearance provided an explicit reason for wanting to protect her.

When Lindsay glanced curiously in her direction, Coral saw that her eyes were a lighter gray than her brother's, but just as sharp and inquisitive. Her black hair was swept back and fastened with a bow in a casual, yet elegant style.

"Are you responsible for the miracle?" Lindsay asked, walking toward Coral. She enunciated her words in a precise, cultured English, though she spoke quickly as though in a rush.

Coral blinked in confusion. "Excuse me?"

The other woman smiled broadly, and Coral noticed she had a slight overbite, which was oddly charming.

"Are you the magician, the miracle worker, the reason why it's possible for someone actually to walk on this carpet without crushing something or needing a tetanus jab? I've always said the love of a good woman could turn him into a respectable human being. I hope you're the one responsible for this astounding transformation."

"I suppose I am, but not quite in the way you mean. My company was hired to bring Outfitters more into the twentieth century." She smiled at Paul briefly before bringing her attention back to his sister. "In Paul's case we also had to adhere to a strict health code when it came to tackling his office."

His sister thoroughly enjoyed Coral's comment, and laughed, as did the man who had just walked into Paul's office. Paul's smile was a little pained.

"Coral," he said, stepping forward, "this is my sister, Lindsay Ellison. Behind her is her husband, Taylor Ellison. They've arrived from England to attend Montego Qui's concert and to make my life miserable." To his sister and brother-in-law he said, "This is Coral Bentley."

Lindsay gave her brother a curious glance before extending her hand.

"How nice to meet you," she said warmly to Coral. "We thought seeing Monty in concert was going to be the most exciting event during our trip to Washington. Then we walk into Paul's office expecting to wade through the usual swamp of papers and find a replica of my great-aunt Beryl's immaculate front room. Did you know, I didn't realize until this afternoon that Paul had commandeered Grandfather's antique desk from the Abbey? It had always been covered in muck before this."

Paul glared at the tall man who had moved closer to his wife. "I thought pregnant women were supposed to be weepy and crave disgusting combinations of food. What is she doing wrong?"

"Not a thing that I can see." Paul's brother-in-law extended his right hand to Coral. "Hello. May I add my words of praise for managing to persuade Paul to shovel out this room?"

"You may." Coral shook his hand. "But I didn't exactly persuade Paul to become more organized. He was out of town at the time. His partner arranged for our work to be done."

Lindsay's gaze rested on her brother, who glared back at her. Then she studied Coral with frank curiosity. "He didn't know you were going to clean his office?"

Coral shook her head.

"And he let you live?" Lindsay asked, awe in her voice and expression.

Taylor chuckled, but Paul stepped forward to take his sister's arm.

Guiding her toward the couch, he said, "I'm sure there is something in the pregnant lady's rule book that says you're not supposed to instigate riots by irritating the hell out of prospective uncles. Be a good girl and try not to bother us for five minutes. Then I'll let you tell Coral about how I made an army barracks for my tin soldiers out of your dollhouse when I was ten. She'll enjoy the part about me having to come to your dolls' tea party as punishment."

Lindsay sat and gestured for Coral to sit with her. Coral shook her head, though. "I really must be going," she said. "I have a long drive ahead of me."

"Please stay a little longer, Miss Bentley,"

Lindsay said. "I have so many questions I'd like to ask you."

"Please call me Coral."

"All right, Coral, and you must use my Christian name as well. I wish you would stay for a few moments more. Those two are going to discuss Paul's pet project, and I would rather talk with you than listen to them. Since we are here for such a brief time, this is the only opportunity Paul and Taylor are going to have to discuss Tripod. It won't be possible for them to go over the papers Taylor brought with him tonight since we're dining with friends. Monty will be arriving tomorrow morning and will expect us all to spend Saturday with him before we attend his concert that evening. We return to England on Sunday."

Coral sorted through all that information and grabbed onto the one confusing part. "Tripod?" she repeated.

Lindsay nodded. "Tripod stands for the three supporting branches of a camp that offers training classes in art, music, and sports to underprivileged children. There are also three men who head the foundation—Paul, Taylor, and our older brother, Reggie."

The picture of Paul Forge as a pleasure-seeking rascal was fading, replaced with a man who had much more substance than she'd at first thought. Coral sat down on the couch, thoughts of leaving temporarily set aside.

"So you and your husband are only here for a short time," she said.

"Unlike Paul," Lindsay answered, "we've remained in England. We mainly live in Taylor's ancestral manse in Buckinghamshire about thirty miles northeast of London. We also have a flat in London for convenience when his work requires his presence for any length of time. After the baby comes, I'll probably be staying in the country more rather than hop back and forth as we do now."

"What type of work does your husband do?"

"He is affiliated with the Royal Philharmonic Concert Orchestra, mainly in an administrative capacity, luckily for me, which doesn't require him to travel with the orchestra when they perform away from England. Occasionally he manages to put his many years of piano training to use by arranging some of the musical scores," she added with obvious pride.

Even though she should be leaving for the trip to her parents' home, Coral couldn't bring herself to go just yet. She had been surrounded by gifted, talented people her whole life but not often in the creative arts. She was also learning more about Paul that she found as intriguing as he was.

"From what Paul has said, I got the impression you all know Montego Qui well. Is this trip business or pleasure, or a combination of both?"

Lindsay smiled. "More like a command performance. Monty doesn't perform in the States all that often for the simple reason that he hates to fly. He prefers remaining in Madrid. He reluctantly boards an airplane for the few concerts he agrees to play elsewhere. It's not general knowledge, but this will be his last public concert. We didn't want to miss it. Are you familiar with his work?"

"Yes. I'm a big fan. I tried to get tickets for this concert from the moment they went on sale, but I wasn't able to get any."

Lindsay glanced at her husband, who was deep in conversation with Paul near her brother's desk. Lowering her voice, she leaned toward Coral and said, "Monty is going to surprise Taylor by playing one of his original compositions. It took a great deal of persuasion on Paul's part and some pregnant-wife cajoling to get Taylor to agree to come. July is a busy schedule for the orchestra, but as you can see, we managed to get him here."

Coral now understood another reason why Paul had been so anxious to locate the tickets. She lifted her gaze to look at Paul as he concentrated on a document his brother-in-law had given him. She had formed her earlier opinion of him with little to go on except her own imagination. The real person was proving to be much more interesting—and dangerously appealing.

Paul happened to glance up at that instant and saw that both women were watching him.

Coral looked seriously puzzled about something, and he sensed it had to do with him. He could understand the feeling. He wasn't all that clear in his own mind about the effect she had on him.

Then he saw his sister's expression, and his blood froze. She had that brooding look in her eyes that could only mean trouble. And usually for him. Whatever Lindsay was planning, he'd better nip it in the bud before she set his progress with Coral back a decade or two.

He bent over the desk and signed the last page of the agreement Taylor had given him, then handed the papers back to his brother-in-law. "I agree with Reggie that we should take the option and see what kind of offer the estate agent comes up with before we look somewhere else. It's the best location we've found yet. Now we'd better tend to the women before they get restless and come after us with whips and chairs."

"I didn't realize you were into that sort of thing, old boy," Taylor said with a grin as he put the papers away in a battered leather satchel.

"I'm talking about a tongue-lashing from your dear wife, and Coral will suggest I sit up straight in my chair. She has this tidy side of her nature that can be intimidating."

"You don't seem to be suffering too badly," Taylor remarked. "How long have you been seeing her?"

"Who?"

"Don't play dumb with me. Ever since I walked in here, I've seen you looking at her every three minutes to make sure she hasn't disappeared like a puff of smoke. I've been there, you know, when I met your sister. I know the signs."

"Don't be daft," Paul said, then found himself looking in Coral's direction again just as Taylor had said he did. He glanced back at his brother-in-law, and there was a hint of alarm in his voice when he muttered, "I've barely even kissed her or . . . anything else. Yet it doesn't seem to matter. I feel like I'm coming down with a fever when I'm with her."

"You are." Taylor grinned again. "You know, your sister called me a bloody fool when she met me. I'd nearly run over her when I left a car park. It doesn't always happen with a bolt of lightning or fireworks. Sometimes it takes radical steps, such as running them down with your car or putting up with their peculiar traits, such as being neat, that would otherwise drive you crazy."

"Well, it will pass, so bugger off."

Paul felt better for having said it aloud. His brother-in-law had implied that he had fallen for Miss Shipshape-and-Bristol-Fashion Coral Bentley, which was hardly the case.

He saw Coral smile when she looked up and found him staring at her. Again.

An ice-cold sliver of panic insinuated itself

along his spine. He could admit he found her oddly intriguing, but then he was curious about a number of unusual occurrences in nature. That didn't mean he cared about them. He only found them interesting.

Too late he realized his sister was talking to him. And looking like the cat who'd licked up all the cream. It was really disgusting to see that smug look on her face.

"What?" he asked when she called his name as though he was trying her patience beyond endurance.

"I think it's a smashing idea," Lindsay said. "What do you think?"

"About what?"

Exasperation oozed from Lindsay's every pore. "I knew you weren't listening. Honestly, Paul. Do try to hone in on what I'm saying if you please. Watch my lips if it helps."

Paul stepped closer and made an exaggerated point of staring at her mouth, so that Lindsay giggled.

Taylor intervened. "Lindsay has asked Coral if she wanted to go with us to Monty's concert as our guest. We do have that extra ticket."

"Monty sent that other ticket," Paul said, "in case I wanted to bring someone, rather than be a third wheel with the two of you."

"So have you asked someone else to go with you?" his sister asked.

"No."

"Then why can't Coral come along with us? She's an avid fan of Monty's and hasn't been able to get tickets to see him. This very well might be his last concert, which means she will never get another chance. I, for one, think she should be rewarded for taking on the task of making a silk purse out of a sow's ear, so to speak."

"I didn't say she couldn't come with us," Paul pointed out. "But I prefer to make my own arrangements. Why don't you two go for a stroll, and I'll approach her on the subject in my own charming way?"

Smiling warmly at Coral, Lindsay sprang to her feet. "Oh, good. See you tomorrow night, then."

Coral opened her mouth to protest the plans that seemed to be including her without her consent. She would have said something, too, if her audience hadn't left the room. Taylor gave her a parting smile, and Lindsay waved her hand as they sailed out the door, leaving her alone with Paul.

He sat down beside her and placed his arm casually across the back of the couch, his hand only inches from her hair. "Well, what do you think?"

"About what?"

"Going to the concert."

"With you?"

"No. The bloody Prince of Wales," he said

impatiently. "Of course with me. And Lindsay and Taylor." When she started shaking her head, he asked, "Why not? I thought you were so desperate to see Monty."

Coral studied him for half a minute. His expression revealed his lack of pleasure in her response. He really thought he only had to dangle Montego Qui like a juicy carrot in front of her and she would be led wherever he wanted her to go.

Part of the problem in saying no was that the Spanish guitarist was a very tempting carrot. The other part was that she would like to see Paul again without her work being the reason. Or his sister prodding him into offering the invitation.

The truth was the only answer she could give.

"You already know I'm a stickler about things being neat and tidy. Maybe you don't realize that this carries over into my private life too. It makes me crazy if something is discarded carelessly before someone is through with it. For instance I wouldn't like to be the cause of some poor woman crying into her pillow tomorrow night because you won't be taking her to the concert as she expected."

Paul tilted his head to one side and asked curiously, "Are you asking if I'm involved with someone?"

"No, I'm asking you to take whoever you

would have arranged to take. You've been pressured by your sister into including me. As much as I would like to see Montego Qui, I wouldn't enjoy the concert knowing you would have taken someone else if Lindsay had given you a choice." She gathered up her purse and adjusted the strap over her shoulder as she stood. "Besides I have plans for the weekend."

Paul got to his feet. "What sort of plans?"

"My plans," she said unhelpfully.

Stepping around the low table in front of the couch, she started walking toward the door. Paul stopped her with a hand on her arm. With his other hand he held out one of the tickets.

She looked down at the strip of paper. "What am I supposed to do with that?"

"Use it or don't. It's yours." When she didn't take it, he said seriously, "I would like you to go to the concert, Coral. If you don't like the idea of going with me, just pretend you don't know me when you sit down."

She heard the sincerity in his voice. Honestly, she thought with exasperation, for an intelligent man he could be as thick as the Great Wall of China.

"I don't object to going to the concert with you," she explained. "But I prefer to be asked for reasons other than that a man's sister forced the invitation on him."

When she turned back toward the door, Paul put his hand on the side of her neck. Heat that had nothing to do with temperature flowed up his arm. He saw by the way her eyes widened in surprise that she had felt something too.

"I've handled this badly," he admitted. His gaze went to the soft hollow of her throat, where he could feel her heartbeat accelerate under his thumb. "I would like you to attend the concert because you would enjoy seeing Monty perform and because I would like to see you again, this time out of either your office or mine and for personal reasons that have nothing to do with business."

"Be honest, Paul. Would you have thought of asking me if your sister hadn't put you on the spot?"

"I don't expect you to believe it, but it did cross my mind as I was searching through the files earlier. You'll have to take my word that I haven't arranged to take anyone else, but giving you such short notice seemed in bad taste. Considering your reaction just now, I wasn't wrong in guessing you would have been offended."

Coral decided this was one of those no-win situations involving basic irreconcilable differences between male and female brain waves. How he asked her was more important to her than why he wanted her to go to the concert, but he was never going to understand that.

She had a choice. She could refuse out of principle, or she could accept the lopsided, last-minute invitation and spend an evening with an attractive rascal while enjoying the unforgettable music created by a legend.

She reached out and plucked the ticket from his hand. "If you give even the slightest hint of a smug smile," she warned, "I'll tear this up."

"My mother raised a gentleman, remember? I wouldn't do anything so crass." Still Paul had trouble concealing how pleased he was that she had accepted. He took back the ticket. "We might as well go the whole way. I'll come for you about seven."

Coral opened her purse and removed a small notebook. She jotted down her address, then tore off the sheet and handed it to him.

"What about your plans for the weekend?" he asked.

"They appear to have changed," she said as she walked toward the door. "I'll see you at seven tomorrow evening."

Paul wanted to stop her from leaving, although he couldn't think of a good reason other than that he didn't want her to go. But he had the consolation of knowing he would see her the next night.

It wasn't until several minutes had passed that he realized she hadn't said what her weekend plans were that she was changing. Evidently whatever she was doing wasn't so important that she couldn't postpone it for an evening. The desire to know who she was seeing, what she did on her own away from her business, and where she would be was stronger than it should have been, and he didn't know why. It was odd that he felt he knew her so well, yet he realized he barely knew her at all. He would recognize her scent in a room full of other women, hear only her voice in a crowd, want only her out of a bevy of beautiful women.

He was as sure of all that as he was of his own name, but he didn't know why this particular woman attracted him so strongly.

For a man who usually knew where he was going and why, with Coral he was fumbling around in foreign territory without a map.

FIVE

When her doorbell rang Saturday night, Coral was talking on the telephone. She told her mother not to hang up, that she would be right back after she answered the door. She set the receiver down on an end table before her mother could ask whom she was expecting.

Paul had anticipated that the evening with Coral would be a unique experience, although not necessarily from the moment she opened the door.

She gestured for him to come inside and whirled around, leaving him standing in her doorway. For a few seconds he simply stared as she crossed the carpeted floor in stockinged feet.

The professional woman had been replaced by a vision in black and gold. She wore a gold silk tank top under a black crepe jacket that had been trimmed in embroidered gold leaves down the front and across the shoulders. Her black skirt ended just above the knee, allowing him a tantalizing view of her fabulous legs.

He watched as she picked up a phone receiver off the table next to a high-backed chair and faced him. She smiled, then said, "I'm back," to the person on the line.

Gold earrings gleamed against the backdrop of her brown hair, which had somehow increased in volume. Even her face had transformed in some subtle way. Rather than a serious businessperson, he was looking at an exciting, attractive woman ready for a night out.

As he stepped into the living room, Paul's gaze was drawn to the furnishings of her apartment. The fact that her home was neat didn't surprise him, but her choice of colors did. Instead of playing it safe with creams and tans, she had chosen a symphony of purple, soft greens, yellow, and white. The room was small and cozy and intimate, and he felt the warmth of it drawing him in.

The living room adjoined a dining area, off of which was what he assumed was the kitchen, since he could see a refrigerator next to a partition that jutted several feet across the open space. A hallway led off the living room, apparently to her bedroom.

He walked over to look at a painting hanging over the sofa while he waited for her to finish her call. As a rule he didn't care for abstract paintings. He liked a tree to look like a tree, but this entire canvas was filled with waves of muted, yet vibrant colors that made him think of distant mountains and misty mornings.

Since she was only a few feet away, he couldn't help overhearing Coral's side of the phone conversation, which he found unusual, to say the least.

"How can he have a list already? I just left a couple of hours ago." After a brief hesitation she continued, "I told Pop that the lumber for the supers couldn't be delivered until Tuesday. Short of cutting down a tree himself, he doesn't have any choice but to wait unless he wants to go into town and pick it up himself. No, I didn't think he would. Assure him that I won't forget to bring the new queens next weekend to replace the two that died. If he would have the mail delivered to the farm, he could have them sooner." After a pause Coral said, "I really have to go, Mom. I'll call you in the middle of the week as usual."

Paul turned when he heard her replace the receiver. "So, visiting your parents were your plans for the weekend?"

"Hmmm," she murmured as she picked up a gold bracelet from the table.

"How often do you manage to see them?"

She wrapped the bracelet around her wrist. "I try to get home every weekend. It's not always possible and causes some problems if I can't make it. Leaving early today disturbed the routine."

"Where do they live?"

"Outside of Charlottesville."

"That's over a two-hour drive from here."

"I'm aware of every mile."

When he saw she was having difficulty with the clasp of the bracelet, he said, "I'll do that for you."

Coral held the linked chain and her arm out to him. He fastened the clasp on the first attempt.

"Another of your many talents, I see," she said lightly.

"The benefits of growing up with a sister. I've learned to fasten all sorts of feminine folderol over the years." He slid his fingers around her wrist and held her arm out so that he could see her without anything obstructing his view.

"You look lovely, Miss Bentley," he said. "I will be proud to have you arrive on my arm."

"Why, thank you, Mr. Forge." She glanced at his black tuxedo, immaculate white pleated shirt, and black cummerbund and formal tie. "You're quite stunning yourself."

"You are too kind," he said smoothly. He glanced down at her feet. "I rather like you without shoes."

She smiled. "That's an odd compliment. And a curious one."

"You aren't quite as intimidating without high heels."

"Intimidating?" She was shocked. "I'm the least intimidating person I know."

"You must not know many people." He dropped her hand. "Hop into your pretty dancing slippers so that we can be on our way. If we're late, Monty will pout."

"Wait a minute. You can't call me intimidating and then drop it."

"Sure I can if we're going to be late for Monty's concert. I don't mind if you go without shoes, but the people at the door might not feel the same way." He made a slight bow. "Your carriage awaits."

His carriage turned out to be a dark blue Jaguar, which he drove with consummate skill in the heavy traffic. Coral sat back to enjoy the benefit of being a passenger, a rare occurrence.

In case she never had another opportunity, she asked about the camp his sister had mentioned. "Tell me about Tripod."

He gave her a brief glance. "Lindsay has been her usual chatty self, I see. Since I don't know what she told you, I don't know what you want to know."

"She said you, your brother, and her husband have formed an organization that helps underprivileged children. I was curious how that came about."

He didn't answer immediately. In the light

reflected from the dash and from the other cars, she could see he was frowning. She felt oddly hurt that he was hesitant to tell her something that was obviously important to him.

Finally he said, "I can speak three languages fluently, but I can't think of any words to make what happened less ugly. It's not a pretty story."

Coral didn't push or prod. He either wanted to confide in her or he didn't.

When he did speak a minute later, his words were blunt and to the point. "Taylor had a sister who was raped and badly beaten by a group of teenagers when she was fourteen. She eventually recovered from her physical injuries, but she couldn't deal with the emotional aftermath. She committed suicide on her fifteenth birthday."

"Dear God!"

"Taylor and his family were devastated, as you can imagine. My family have been friends and neighbors of the Ellisons for as long as I can remember. The two families had spent a lot of time together over the years, and we were aware how the tragedy was affecting them."

Coral thought of her niece—feisty, funny eight-year-old Sally—and felt nauseous.

"The boys were never caught," Paul continued, "and the family had no outlet for their anger and hatred for the people who could commit such a horrendous act. Marina was dead and the boys responsible hadn't been punished. Taylor and his parents needed to find a positive way to overcome their grief, to take some type of action toward preventing any other young girl from having her innocence stolen from her and possibly her life. Taylor's father would have been happy to lock up every lad from ten to twenty as a precaution, but since that wasn't possible, something else had to be done. It was my father's suggestion that we do what we could to change the environment that created the type of individual who could commit a violent act.''

"So Tripod provides an alternative to crime by directing underprivileged teenagers' energies toward sports and music?"

Paul nodded. "The activities are used as an outlet for young people who could easily choose the wrong direction unless they see they have an alternative. Tripod stresses sports and the arts as an incentive to get an education. We provide tutors to help those who are struggling with certain subjects, which are almost all of them at first. Every child has to make an effort to get his or her schooling. We don't require that they maintain the highest levels, but they do have to try. If they do what is expected of them, they gain self-respect, a sense of achievement, and the right to participate in our sports and music programs."

"If you make the dessert tempting enough, they will eat their Brussels sprouts."

Paul chuckled. "Something like that. So far we've had an eighty-nine-percent success rate.

We naturally would like that figure to be higher, but that's up to the kids."

"That's eighty-nine percent who are working toward a future for themselves instead of taking away someone else's."

She had been looking ahead when she'd spoken, but when she felt Paul's gaze on her profile, she looked at him. "Did I say something wrong?"

He shook his head and brought his gaze back to the road. "Your ability to cut through the chaff is remarkable."

Coral noticed he had the same expression on his face as he'd had earlier when he had commented on her bare feet. "And intimidating?"

"Neither statement is meant to be an insult. I can usually put most people into categories, but you are an exception. It puzzles me."

Shifting in her seat to face him, she asked, "Why do you put people into categories?"

"Most people do in one way or another."

"Why would they?"

"Habit."

Coral felt it was more than that. Having a compulsion to label people wasn't something someone decided to do. Usually the decision was made for a person because of some event or incident. A man didn't erect a protective shield unless he felt he needed it. Why Paul Forge felt it was necessary to be on guard was only one of many questions she'd like answers to eventually.

Instead of being a lightweight, thrill-seeking jock, Paul was more like a slab of solid granite. He wasn't perfect. There were cracks and fissures to be investigated and examined and acknowledged, along with a polished surface that could deceive an undiscerning eye from recognizing the depth of his strength. When someone wanted to shove him in a direction he didn't want to go, he would stand firm and not be moved from his position.

They were about ten minutes away from their destination when Paul said, "I might not get another chance this evening to ask you something that's been driving me crazy."

"We certainly wouldn't want that to happen," she said with amusement. "What do you want to ask me?"

"I couldn't help overhearing your conversation with your mother. I've tried to figure out what you meant when you told her you were sending a couple of queens to replace the ones that died, but it escapes me completely."

Coral smiled broadly. "I never thought how it would sound to someone who didn't know my family. My father is an entomologist, someone who studies insects. At the moment he's involved in several experiments with bees. Each hive has to have a queen bee to be productive, and he needs replacements."

"What a relief," Paul said with a smile. "My

imagination had gone in several other directions.
Can bees really be sent through the post?"

Coral answered his question and had time to
tell him more about her family before they arrived at the Kennedy Center. She told him
about her older brother, Guthrie, who created
intricate clocks with mechanical scenes in them
and was usually late for meals because he hadn't
checked the time. He heard about Guthrie's
wife, Nadine, who wrote cookbooks featuring
natural grains and honey. She mentioned her
brother, Harry, a botanist who was developing a
culture to be used to propogate centuries-old
seeds discovered in archaeological excavations.
She also talked about her niece and nephew,
Harry's children, whom he was raising after the
early death of his wife.

When she explained that her family all lived
together on a farm near Charlottesville, Paul
didn't ask why she was the only one not living at
the Fields of Honey. He had a feeling the question would require more time to answer than
they had at the moment.

Once they were seated with Lindsay and
Taylor in four of the best seats in the house,
Paul was pleased he had learned more about the
woman who intrigued him.

He was also aware that the exchange of background information had come solely from Coral.
He was in no rush to divulge his own family history. It always made a difference.

The next couple of hours were pure enchant-
ment for Coral. The opening act was a pleasant
string quartet performing a medley of soothing
songs that prepared the audience for the dramatic style of the famous guitarist. Montego Qui
was more than the excellent musician she had
always admired. He was a natural entertainer, a
charming showman, and an uninhibited showoff.
He held the audience in the palm of his talented
hand with his performance, his repartee, and his
presence, lifting them to greater heights of pleasure than they had ever achieved with his music
alone.

Since she had considered his musical ability
to be somewhat larger than life, Coral was surprised to see Montego was a diminutive man,
perhaps five feet eight inches tall. He was
dressed all in black except for a pleated white
shirt. His coal-black hair, which obviously had
been doctored by a skilled hairstylist, gleamed in
the spotlights as he marched back and forth
across the stage in between musical numbers,
holding his guitar by its neck as though it were a
chicken whose neck he was about to wring. And
wring it he did every time he played.

At one point during his performance
Montego's dark eyes scanned the audience, and
he grinned widely when he saw Paul, Lindsay,
and Taylor, and he included Coral in his nod of
greeting.

The song he played as an encore was a

haunting melody that tore at the heart and then mended it again. Although she thought she had heard all of his recorded performances, Coral was unfamiliar with that particular melody. Beside her, she saw Lindsay clasp her husband's hand, and Coral recalled Lindsay saying Montego Qui was to play one of Taylor's compositions as a surprise.

Montego left his usual position on the stool in the center of the stage and, without missing a single note, sat down on the edge of the stage directly in front of Taylor. For a man of his advanced years, this should have been awkward, but it was done with apparent ease and a great deal of style.

Coral heard Lindsay sniffle indelicately and glanced her way, not at all surprised to see several tears gliding down the woman's cheeks. Between the soulful strumming of the guitar strings and the sight of Lindsay's hand being crushed in her husband's, Coral was feeling the emotion of the moment too.

She groped blindly for Paul's hand. Even if she could have taken her eyes away from Montego to look for his hand, she wouldn't have been able to see past her own tears.

When he guessed what she wanted, Paul turned his hand over and clasped Coral's palm against his, threading his fingers through hers. He looked at her and smiled when he saw the tears glittering in her eyes.

As he watched the play of emotions on her face, something tender, yet fierce in its intensity, tightened in his chest.

Thundering applause announced the finish of Montego's encore, and the performer returned to his former position on the stage. Gesturing for silence, he stood in front of the microphone and waited until the enthusiastic crowd contained their appreciation long enough for him to speak.

He announced that the composer of the piece he'd just performed was in the audience, and he would like the audience to show their appreciation to him. A spotlight was suddenly aimed at the area where they were seated. Montego not only introduced Taylor but also the people he was with.

Coral blinked and sat frozen in shock. The bright light had nothing to do with it once Montego announced names and titles. Not complimentary adjectives, but real titles.

Taylor was introduced as Viscount Ravenswood, Taylor Ellison, his wife as Lady Lindsay Ellison, who was the sister of Lord Paul Denton-Forge, son of the Earl of Tysdale, who was present with his guest, Miss Coral Bentley.

The applause was deafening. Lindsay and Taylor stood to acknowledge the introduction, and Coral numbly obeyed the pressure of Paul's hand as he drew her along with him when he got to his feet.

Coral was dimly aware of the clapping hands,
but she only heard the echo of Montego Qui's
voice announcing the titles of the people she was
with.

The scar over an old wound had been ripped
off with remarkable ease by only a few words.
Coral thought she'd gotten over the feeling of
being out of step with those she was with, but
the all-too-familiar awkwardness was back. Being an average duckling in a family of genius
swans had required a number of compromises
on her part over the years in order for her to
find a place for herself. She had worked hard to
fit into her own niche, where she was accepted
for herself and not judged by the achievements
of her exceptionally gifted family.

Noting Coral's unease, Paul assumed she
wasn't comfortable being in the limelight. She
stood stiffly beside him, staring at Montego,
who was grinning like a proud father showing
off his brood. She'd withdrawn her hand from
his once they were standing, and resembled a
statue. Paul cursed himself for not warning her
that he'd talked to Montego earlier in the day
and had given the performer the name of the
woman he was bringing. He'd thought she
would enjoy the surprise. Evidently he had mis-
calculated.

He bent his head and spoke close to her ear
so that she could hear him over the applause that
showed no signs of letting up.

"It'll be over in a few minutes. Then we'll go backstage and see Montego."

If that was supposed to make Coral feel better, it fell short of succeeding.

The applause didn't subside until Montego finally walked off the stage, and it was obvious he wouldn't return no matter how enthusiastically they clapped and cheered. A general restlessness came over the crowd as they gathered up their programs and belongings to leave the concert hall.

When Paul reached the end of their row, a man in a tuxedo gestured for the group to follow him. Paul put his hand under Coral's arm and led the way to a concealed door that led backstage.

Monty was in his element in his dressing room, accepting the accolades with accustomed ease and obvious pleasure. Coral was surprised to discover he was an outrageous flirt, kissing her hand, her cheek, and giving her a hug that bordered on shameless.

The affection between Paul, Lindsay, Taylor, and Monty was genuine and of long standing, she noticed. They knew a number of the same people and talked easily about places and events they had in common. Occasionally Monty said something in French or Spanish that had everyone laughing. Except Coral, who hadn't understood a word. She felt even more alienated than before.

Earlier, she had looked forward to getting to know Paul better during the evening, and she had gotten her wish. She now knew he was the son of an earl, spoke French and Spanish, and was as rich as Croesus. And she hadn't learned any of those things from him.

She overheard Monty tell Paul and Lindsay that he had recently visited their parents at their villa in France. They were enjoying their retirement after turning the family estate, Tysdale Abbey, over to Reggie, the heir to his father's title and the extensive estate in Buckinghamshire County.

Coral made the connection between the famous high-quality pottery she'd heard of and Paul's family, when Monty mentioned that Tysdale pottery was now available on the international market thanks to Reggie's management.

As more people pushed into the dressing room eager to see Monty, Coral was separated from Paul in the crush. He had held her securely at his side with one arm around her waist, until he had to rescue Lindsay from being bashed in the head when someone attempted to pass a guitar over the crowd for Monty to sign. Coral was gradually elbowed out of the pack and ended up outside the room without sustaining any major bruising. Several reporters glanced at her hopefully, then shifted their attention back to the doorway when they didn't recognize her as someone important or famous.

Feeling like a salmon trying to swim up-stream, Coral struggled through the mass of people waiting to catch a glimpse of the star performer or perhaps even get the opportunity to meet the famous guitarist. She could imagine their reactions if these people knew they had witnessed his last concert in the United States. She certainly wasn't about to tell them. She wanted to get out of there alive and relatively unscathed by jabbing elbows and shoes of all sizes trodding on her feet.

She glimpsed an exit sign ahead and aimed for it with a determination brought on by the desperate need for fresh air and more than a few inches of space. Finally she managed to step out a side door. For a few seconds she closed her eyes and enjoyed the relative silence and the ability to move without bumping into someone.

Since she couldn't stay where she was forever, she thought about her options. She could search for Paul's car and wait for him there, but she'd have to stand around like an idiot, since he had locked the doors. She didn't fancy the idea of fighting her way back to Monty's dressing room through the obstacle course she'd just escaped from. As a last resort she could hail a taxi and make her own way home.

All things considered, she went with the third option.

An hour later when her security buzzer rang several times, Coral tightened the belt of her robe and answered it. As she expected, Paul replied to her query by saying, "You know damn well who it is. Let me in."

Although she could have done without a confrontation that night, she pressed the button to release the lock on the lobby door downstairs. Then she walked into the kitchen alcove to put a kettle of water on to boil. Looking through her wide selection of tea, she chose chamomile. If there was any time for the soothing effects of an herbal tea, this was it.

She should have expected Paul would wonder where she had gone, but she'd thought he would phone to make sure she had gotten home all right. After all, Lord Paul Denton-Forge had been brought up to be a gentleman.

She glanced down at the ordinary cotton robe she'd put on shortly after arriving home. He was going to have to take her as she was. And in more ways than the way she was dressed.

The water hadn't started to boil when she heard knuckles rapping on her door. Resigned, she straightened her shoulders and left the kitchen to answer the summons.

When she opened the door, she immediately noticed his altered appearance from the last time she'd seen him. The top few buttons on his shirt had been undone and his black tie hung loose around his neck. His hair was rumpled and his eyes burned into hers.

She didn't move aside so that he could enter, nor did she invite him in. As politely as she could, she said, "You didn't need to stop by to see if I got home all right. A phone call would have accomplished the same thing, but since you have, I'd like to thank you for letting me use your extra ticket." Her mouth twisted into a rueful smile. "The evening was unforgettable."

"Is leaving in the middle of a date some rude American custom I'm not familiar with?"

"We didn't have a date," she said, taking offense at his question. "You had an extra ticket, and I used it." She stepped back automatically when he moved forward. "What are you doing?"

Instead of answering her he showed her. Her feet were suddenly several inches off the floor as he lifted her with remarkable ease and entered her apartment. He set her down after he was inside, then closed the door and stepped around her. He tossed his tuxedo jacket over the back of a chair and stood in the middle of the living room, his gaze on her.

The high-pitched whistle on her teakettle was a welcome interruption. Without speaking, she calmly walked into the small kitchen and removed the kettle from the burner.

Paul followed her as far as the partition that

separated the kitchen from the dining area, and she greatly appreciated that. Before the events of that evening, the close confines of her tiny kitchen could have created some interesting possibilities with Paul. Now his closeness would only cause her to feel more awkward than she already felt.

She measured three teaspoons of loose tea into a pot and poured the boiling water into it, then took two cups out of the cupboard.

"If that other cup is for me, you can put it back," Paul said. "I don't drink tea."

"Another misconception I've made about you," she said as she returned the cup to the cupboard. "They are beginning to pile up."

He leaned against the partition and crossed his arms over his chest. "What other misconceptions have you had about me?"

"There are too many to mention."

"Try."

She gave him a blank look but didn't take the bait. Opening the refrigerator, she bent down to get a lemon from the crisper drawer. Belatedly she realized she was giving him a nice view of her backside with it.

"Where did you go?" Paul asked, his voice unusually husky.

Coral quickly straightened. "I thought that was obvious," she replied as she cut a wedge out of the lemon. She made a big production out of pouring her tea, squeezing the lemon into it, then stirring in a teaspoon of honey. "I came home."

"Before that. Something happened after Monty's encore. One minute you were squeezing my hand as though you would never let go, then the spotlight was turned on us, and you looked as though you'd been given some nasty medicine."

"I'm shy," she murmured, and took a sip of the tea as she watched him over the rim.

It was the wrong time to be sarcastic. He moved so suddenly, she didn't have time to step out of his way. He took the cup and saucer out of her hand, and they clattered dangerously as he set them onto the counter.

Then she had other concerns more pressing than the condition of her china.

His fingers clasped her upper arms to hold her in front of him. "Apparently you're under another misconception about me. You might think I treat everything lightly because I'm in the business of arranging holidays for people for fun and recreation, but I don't play games in my private life."

"Of course you do," she said matter-of-factly. "You play Blindman's Buff and Keep-away like a pro."

Paul stared at her. "What are you talking about?"

"How about Let's Pretend?" she continued. "Let's pretend you are Paul Forge, who can ski, dive out of airplanes, and ride rafts down Devil's Canyon. This Paul Forge has an endearing quality about him that makes people go out of their way to help him with the mundane office chores that seem beyond his comprehension." She twisted out of his hold and took two steps away from him. "Did you have a good laugh when I took your problems seriously? Was it a great story to tell your mates over a drink when you pretended you couldn't find something and the stupid woman actually came running to help you? Did you enjoy describing how you made this woman think you were interested in her for reasons other than her ability to find things in your files?" She didn't give him a chance to answer. Striding out of the kitchen, she walked toward the door. "Next time you play this game, do me a favor and choose another person for your entertainment. I discovered I'm not a very good sport."

She had her hand on the doorknob when Paul caught up with her. "Are you through?"

"Definitely," she snapped as she flung the door open.

He placed the palm of his hand on the door and slammed it shut. "I'm not leaving just yet." He took her hand and led her over to the sofa. "You've had your say. Now it's my turn."

Coral sat down and wished he would do the same. He was towering over her like a dark thundercloud. "So say your piece, Mr. Denton-Forge. Or am I supposed to call you my lord?"

"Call me Paul. That's my name." He took several steps away from her and turned back. "Is that what this is all about? Because you found out my family has a few titles lying around?"

"That's part of it."

"Mine is only a courtesy title, and I never use it. I also don't use Denton."

"I noticed. Other people do use it, however. Like Montego Qui did tonight."

"My brother is the Tysdale heir and entitled to everything that goes with it, which is fine with me. I want neither my father's title nor the estate that goes with it. Luckily Reggie does."

"You just don't get it, do you?"

"Obviously not. Why don't you explain it to me."

"My father has won numerous prestigious awards that he doesn't advertise, but they're part of who he is. Your family's history is part of who you are. I didn't like finding out something so vital to your identity from someone else."

"I'm still the person I was before Monty opened his big mouth."

Unable to remain seated while he remained standing over her like some giant monolith, Coral rose from the sofa. He thought she was upset because of his heritage; he thought his family background made a difference to her. How could she make him understand that he could be anything from a ditchdigger to a rocket scientist, and it wouldn't matter? What did matter was she had felt stupid not knowing such a basic piece of information about the man she was with.

And she hated feeling stupid.

"You've been climbing too many mountains, Paul. You let out enough line for the other person to follow only as far as you want them to go. What happens when they get too close? Do you cut the rope?"

Paul studied her expression carefully, his anger draining away as he realized she wasn't upset about what she had found out about him, but the way in which she had found it out.

"I have my reasons for not telling you about my father's title," he began. "Have you ever been judged by standards that you had nothing to do with? Been expected to live up to a code of behavior by complete strangers and so-called friends because your ancestors received a title that's been handed down to people who had to do nothing to earn it other than be born? I was luckier than my older brother. I had a choice. I could have stayed in England and lived off the family income, which even for a second son means I wouldn't starve. But I wanted to be my own person rather than an appendage of Tysdale

Abbey. Perhaps the business John and I have developed isn't as respectable or as important to society as other professions are, but it's ours, something we've worked for that hasn't been handed to us."

The color had drained from Coral's face as he began speaking, then rushed back as he went on, leaving her cheeks flushed. Paul didn't see the changes in her expression, though, because he was walking toward the door.

After opening it, he paused, but he didn't look back at her. "After all this time, you would think I would have learned that people can't separate me from my background."

Coral stared at the door as it closed behind him. The soft click of the latch seemed obscenely loud in the silence of the room, and she realized she'd been holding her breath.

She sank down heavily on the couch and leaned her head back. She'd been looking into a mirror image of coincidence the whole time and had never seen her own reflection. Paul's situation was so similar to hers, she should have recognized it. They each had to deal with the repercussions of their family's accomplishments. They weren't able to live up to such high standards of excellence nor live down their reputations.

Instead of thinking logically, she had let her emotions rule, a major failing in her thought processes from her father's point of view. It was certainly a drawback tonight.

For someone who advertised the ability to make sense out of nonsense, Coral had created a major mess out of her relationship with Paul.

SIX

Bending over to plant her hands on her knees for support, Coral tried to catch her breath. She hoped Paul hadn't started for his morning run at the time his sister said he usually did, even though seeing him was the reason she had come to the park early Monday morning in the first place. The clever idea she had come up with the day before had lost some of its brilliance.

Maybe once she could actually breathe without gasping, she would like the plan again.

She straightened to an upright position and swept several damp strands of hair away from her face. She had a vague idea of the picture she made among the more suitably dressed, experienced jogging enthusiasts passing her right and left. One runner turned and ran backward in front of her, grinning as he faded into the distance.

The seat of her white shorts was grass-stained from sitting on a patch of damp ground the first time she'd stopped to rest.

That had occurred after jogging for only five minutes.

Even though the early-morning air was still cool, her cotton top had absorbed patches of perspiration along with several smudges of dirty handprints from her pulling the wet shirt away from her skin several times. The dirt had come from the ground when she had pushed herself upright the second time she'd stopped to rest.

She had put on her lightweight cotton photographer's vest to have a place to keep her keys, a small canister of Mace, some money, and identification. Somehow the vest felt lumpy and certainly seemed heavier than when she'd first put it on.

She sighed heavily, relieved when her lungs actually worked so that she could. This was not the impression she wanted to make when she apologized to Paul.

When she felt she could walk without staggering or keeling over, she turned around to retrace her steps to her parked car.

Meeting Paul in the park had seemed like a good way to see him after she'd talked to Lindsay on the phone at her hotel on Sunday. Luckily Coral had caught Paul's sister just before she and Taylor left for the airport to return to England. Lindsay had been most cooperative after

Coral had asked for Paul's unlisted home phone number. She'd not only given her his number but his address and his regular exercise schedule.

Which explained why Coral was in a park at dawn on a Monday morning panting like an overworked water buffalo.

She put her hand to the small of her back and stretched to ease the tension that wasn't entirely due to the unaccustomed exercise. After two restless nights with only snips of sleep, she knew she would never have any peace until she saw Paul and explained why she'd overreacted the night of the concert. He might not understand, but that was the risk she would have to take. She wanted another chance with Paul, another opportunity to find out what was between them.

"Did I miss the marathon?"

Coral groaned inwardly as she recognized the male voice. Turning, she faced Paul, who looked remarkably fit and healthy in a pair of teal polyester shorts and a jacket zipped halfway up the front over a white T-shirt.

"There's no marathon," she said dryly, "but you're just in time for my heart attack."

His mouth curved in amusement, but his eyes were cautious as he looked at her. "I assume this is not your regular exercise time or place."

She swiped her hand across her damp forehead. "My regular exercise consists of walking across the lobby from the elevator to the cafeteria and back again." She glanced around at the other people trotting past them, some red-faced with veins bulging from exertion, others sipping from plastic water bottles without missing a stride. "There's a whole subculture thing going on here I never knew existed. Do you really enjoy this sort of stuff?"

"Not always," he admitted. "But I like the results, and most of the time I enjoy running. It's a great way to clear out the cobwebs that collect in the brain."

"I've changed my mind," she said flatly, turning back the way she'd been going. "I'm not going to apologize to you after all. We have even less in common than I thought. You are a crazy person."

"There may be more truth in that last statement than I care to think about." This time his smile was more genuine, even reaching his eyes. He took her arm and led her to a bench about thirty feet away on the edge of the walkway. "Who told you where I'd be, Lindsay or John?"

"Lindsay. I managed to catch her before they left for England."

"Lindsay and Taylor left around noon yesterday," he commented. "Which means you've had all this time to think up an approach, and pretending to be a jock was what you came up with. That's very sweet."

"If you had stuck around Saturday night instead of disappearing in a huff, you would have heard my apology then."

Paul studied her face, his outward expression unchanged while inside, taut nerve endings were finally settling down after their blowout Saturday evening.

He wondered what Coral would say if he told her he had planned to come to her office later that day to apologize to her.

When they reached the bench, he gestured for her to sit, then sat down beside her. "So far your plan is working. You found me, and I'm listening. Go ahead."

"Go ahead and what?"

"Apologize. You said that's what you came to the park to do."

"I did apologize."

"When?"

"A few minutes ago. I said if you had stayed Saturday night, you would have heard my apology."

"Well, I didn't stay, so I can hear it now."

Coral found it incredibly difficult to say the words. She looked at him, her gaze caught by the intense expression in the depths of his eyes.

She wished she could read his mind. She couldn't, though, so she'd have to take a chance and tell him what was on hers.

"This is going to sound stupid, and I hate appearing stupid."

"Most people do."

She sighed. "Most people don't have it practically tattooed on their foreheads. From the first day of school on."

Paul frowned. "You're going to have to explain what you mean."

"When Montego first introduced you as someone other than the person I thought I knew, I found myself falling into an old pattern of feeling left out, excluded from everyone around me. I was eight years old again sitting at the dinner table listening to my family and their guests discuss the latest results of an experiment on the digestive system of the rhinoceros beetle."

"The what?"

"*That's* what *I* thought at the time, but I knew better than to ask. Your title itself had nothing to do with my reaction to Montego's introduction. I'm not familiar enough with the British peerage system to have it matter." She lifted her chin a fraction. "It was not knowing something so basic about you that made me feel stupid. It's a feeling I grew up with and evidently haven't grown out of as much as I thought I had."

Her hands were clenched together between her thighs, and Paul reached over and eased them apart. Taking possession of her right hand, he ran his thumb over the smooth fingernails and slender bones of each finger in turn.

After a few moments he asked, "Why in the

world would you feel stupid? You're one of the most intelligent, bright women I've ever met."

"In my family I am a dim bulb in a box of powerful spotlights," she said with a half smile. "I don't have a doctorate in anything, much less two or three. I haven't written a heavy intellectual tome or had dozens of articles accepted in a variety of scholarly journals. Along with all his other awards my father was nominated for a Nobel Prize a few years ago, and my brother, Harry, undoubtedly will be awarded something eventually for his work in photosynthesis or his development of transmutation cultures of ancient seeds."

Paul whistled softly under his breath. "You don't say?"

"Oh, but I do. My mother's specialty is research, which makes her a valuable assistant for my father and brothers. At last count Guthrie has eleven patents for clock mechanisms." She took a breath. "And that is only a brief synopsis of their accomplishments. My call to fame growing up was breaking things; both wrists on separate occasions, my collarbone, an ankle, and two ribs, all before I was sixteen. I stopped vying for attention around then when it occurred to me that I might accidentally kill myself next time I climbed a tree or walked across the barn roof."

Paul continued tracing the shape of her hand. He liked touching her, especially now after he'd thought he might never be able to see or get close to her again. He wanted her to be familiar with his hands on her skin, to be aware of him in every cell in her body.

He hadn't heard her formally apologize as yet, but what he was hearing was fascinating. "You said once that we have nothing in common. We have more in common than you think. The accomplishments of our parents has affected the way we both live our lives. Since we couldn't compete on their level, we made our own way completely apart from them."

"You're right," she said thoughtfully. "We wouldn't be the people we are today if we hadn't worked to overcome our hang-ups. We both could have lived off the reflected glory of our families. Others have." She turned her hand over to thread her fingers through his. "I'm sorry I overreacted Saturday night, Paul. I'm sorry I touched a sensitive nerve. You will have your revenge if you can't forgive me."

He leaned forward. His mouth was only inches away from hers when he said, "I forgive you. Now it's your turn to forgive me. I'm sorry I walked out before we could straighten things out between us."

Even though she hadn't been running this time, Coral was having trouble breathing normally again. The scent of his skin, a combination of soap, shaving lotion, and his own male essence, floated around her, tantalizing her and tempting her. She gave in to her curiosity and placed her hand along his firm jawline. His skin was smooth and warm.

He cupped the back of her neck and covered her cool lips with his own.

Excitement, desire, and anticipation combined into a blend of sensations that made Coral greedy for more. A feeling of pure exhilaration swept over her as he slanted his mouth over hers and deepened the kiss. She clenched her fingers in the material of his jacket and hung on as she sank into the unexpected sensual depths waiting for her.

The sound of a shrill wolf whistle penetrated the heated urgency that had claimed Paul the moment he'd felt her lips under his. When he realized what the sound was, he lifted his head. A jogger was grinning at them as he sprinted by, making an "okay" with gesture with his forefinger and thumb.

Paul automatically shielded Coral by tucking her face against his shoulder. He swallowed a groan of frustration as his aroused body protested against the interruption.

Bending his head, he said, "It looks like I owe you another apology."

Her breath was warm and moist against his skin when she answered. "Please don't say you're sorry you kissed me. I couldn't stand that."

With his finger under her chin, he applied enough pressure to make her look at him. "The apology is for starting something we can't finish. At least not at the moment." He shook his head in mock censure. "You have a dangerous effect on me, lady. I'm a bit old to be necking on a park bench."

"I didn't know there was an age limit for this sort of thing."

Paul didn't respond to the teasing remark. Instead he stared into her eyes with a burning intensity. "You've got me so tied up into knots, I'm not sure I'll ever be free of them."

Coral suddenly felt as though the next few moments might very well be the most important of her life.

"I don't want to cause you any pain, Paul. To be honest, I would just as soon not have to suffer any myself." She pushed against his chest to put a little space between them. "I can walk away now, and you never have to see me again."

His mouth twisted. "Is there another option?"

"You can come to my place for dinner tonight, and we can talk about it."

He moved her hand so that her palm was pressed against his chest where his heart was still beating rapidly. "Talk?"

"Is that your way of saying you want to have an affair with me?"

A corner of his mouth lifted in a slight smile. "This is one situation you can't organize into a neat little file, Coral. I've lived with labels all my life. I'm not about to put one on my relationship with you." He released her and stood. Extending his hand to her, he added, "Let's start with tonight and see what happens."

Accepting his hand, Coral frowned as she got to her feet. "You're doing terrible things to my tightly scheduled, organized existence."

"Good," he said with amusement. "I'd hate to think I'm the only one whose life has been turned upside down. Do you want to run with me since you're here?"

Coral gave him a horrified look. "Not if you want to come to my apartment tonight. I wouldn't be there. I'd be in the hospital."

"I can see I'm going to have to set up a training schedule for you. Where have you parked your car?"

She gestured to her left, but she wanted to discuss his comment about a training schedule. "As I mentioned a minute ago, I come from an exceptionally brainy family, Paul. Their idea of extensive exercise is sharpening a pencil. I'm really not into sweating like you are. I got a stitch in my side the first five minutes I tried running this morning."

He started walking in the direction of her car, taking her arm to coax her along with him since she wasn't doing it on her own.

"We'll take it slow," he said.

Coral wondered whether he was still talking about her training exercise, the walk to the car, or their relationship. She wouldn't worry about that now, she decided. They had another chance to get to know each other better. For now that was more than enough to think about.

She dug out her keys from one of the pockets of her vest when they reached her car. Selecting the correct one, she unlocked the door. Before she opened it, she met Paul's gaze, her expression serious.

"I usually don't chase after men," she said haltingly. "I don't want you to think I make a habit of tracking men down and inviting them to dinner."

"I'm glad you made an exception in my case." He touched the side of her face in a gentle caress. "Just for the record, if you hadn't made a point of seeing me this morning, I was going to barge into your office and demand you agree to give me another chance. If that didn't work, I planned to sweep you into my arms and kiss you until you agreed."

"Darn," she said with a wicked smile. "I'm sorry I missed that."

His eyes were dark with promise. "I'll make it up to you later." He bent his head and kissed her all too briefly but with feeling. His voice was husky as he asked, "Is half past seven tonight all right?"

She nodded, since her ability to breathe had been adversely affected by the restrained sensuality in his kiss. It was a good thing she didn't smoke, she thought ruefully. The way she reacted to Paul's touch, her lungs would never have endured the strain.

He opened the door for her and pushed her gently into the car. "I'll see you tonight," he said, running the back of his finger over her jawline.

After he closed the door, she lowered the window. "Just out of curiosity, how far do you usually run in the park?"

"About five miles."

"Good Lord!"

He grinned. In an imitation of an American accent, he drawled, "You ain't seen nothing yet, lady."

She responded with her version of an English accent. "The mind boggles."

Laughing, Paul stepped away from her car and lifted a hand in a gesture of farewell. Then he turned and set off running at an easy pace.

Coral watched him until he disappeared out of sight. She had never thought of a man in the context of being beautiful, but it was the only adjective she could think of to describe the way Paul moved with an athletic grace that made her mouth go dry.

His penchant for physical exertion was only one of the many things they didn't have in common. Usually she made a list of the pros and cons of any situation that required a commitment, either professionally or personally. This time she didn't plan to make one for fear that the column listing how many differences there were between them would greatly outnumber the similarities.

This was one time in her life when she wasn't able to sort out her feelings into a nice, tidy compartment.

When Paul arrived at her apartment at the appointed time, he didn't come bearing flowers or candy or a book of love sonnets wrapped in a pretty ribbon. He hadn't even brought a bottle of wine.

Coral hadn't been expecting any of those things, but her welcoming smile faltered slightly when she noticed the teal-and-white canvas satchel he was holding at his side. It was oblong and round and obviously full. The bag also reminded her of the exercise outfit he'd worn at the park.

"Are you moving in?" she asked as she closed the door.

"That would be going too fast even for me, although it's a hell of a thought." He held the satchel out to her. "This is for you."

"For me?" she asked in disbelief, then added suspiciously, "Why?"

"Open it," he said with a smile, "and you'll find out."

When she grasped the handle, he released

his grip and she felt the full weight of the bag. "Good grief! What is in here? A bowling ball?"

Chuckling, Paul took the bag from her and carried it into the living room. Setting it down on the sofa, he gestured with his hand.

"Go ahead. Look inside."

With more caution than enthusiasm Coral approached the satchel as though it contained nitroglycerin and the slightest movement would set it off. A heavy zipper ran along the top of the bag. Taking the metal tab in a firm grip, she unzipped the opening and parted the canvas.

What she saw looked harmless enough, until she lifted out the folded garment that lay on top. The material was a shiny nylon, the design similar to the jacket he'd worn that morning in the park. Holding the top in one hand, she took out the matching pair of pants. He'd bought her a jogging suit.

"You shouldn't have," she said softly. She met his gaze. "I mean it. You really shouldn't have."

Paul couldn't help laughing. He knew of no other woman who could amuse him and arouse him at the same time. But there was no denying Coral did both. He was also amazed he'd spent two hours in a sporting goods store shopping for just the right athletic equipment for a woman he was planning to sleep with. He normally would have considered getting her out of her clothes, not buying a unisex outfit.

"There's more," he informed her.

After giving him a look of fatal resignation, she reached into the bag again. This time she drew out a shoe box that contained a pair of white running shoes in her exact size.

"How did you know which size to buy?"

He shrugged. "I guessed."

She hoped his familiarity with women's sizes were due to growing up with a sister and not for other obvious reasons. The jogging outfit had been the correct size too.

The surprises kept coming. There was another box inside the bag. This one was much heavier than the other one. Grasping it with both hands, she sat down and placed the box on her thighs. Taking off the lid, she separated the tissue and stared at the contents. Tentatively she lifted out one of the shiny stainless-steel dumbbells. The bulbous ends were hexagon shaped with a number five engraved on one of them. She took it for granted the other one also weighed five pounds.

She peeked inside the bag one more time and was vastly relieved to find it empty.

"Saying thank you doesn't seem enough somehow," she murmured as she stared at the dumbbells.

Paul smiled and took the weight from her. Placing it back in the box, he returned the box to the satchel along with the shoes and the outfit.

"We'll start tomorrow morning," he said.

"Start what?"

"Your exercise program."

"I don't have an exercise program."

"You will, starting tomorrow morning."

"Paul," she said hesitantly. "I appreciate all these things you bought for me. It was very sweet and generous of you, but I'm not very athletic. I did warn you of that this morning."

"So you did." He set the satchel down on the floor. "You also said something about dinner?"

Pressing her hands on her knees, Coral pushed herself upright. She stepped around the satchel, giving it a baleful glance, and walked toward the small alcove that served as her kitchen.

"Why don't you keep me company while I finish making the salad?"

"I prefer that to sitting on your sofa alone while you're in another room."

She stepped around a corner into the short extension of the L-shaped room. The top of a chopping block situated in the middle of the kitchen was basically the only work space she had. The part of the apartment designated as the kitchen had been an afterthought by the owner, who had turned one larger apartment into two smaller units. In order to make space for the stove and refrigerator, something had to be sacrificed and that had turned out to be cupboards and counters. The man who'd designed the renovations obviously ate out a lot.

As Coral began slicing a tomato for the salad, Paul leaned against the refrigerator and watched her deft movements. A delicious aroma filled the air and literally made his mouth water. The fragrance reminded him of walking past restaurants in Naples until he couldn't stand it anymore and entered one of them for a meal.

Coral might be a stranger to a gymnasium, he thought, but it was clear she was on friendly terms with a kitchen.

"How did you know I like Italian food?" he asked.

She gave him the same answer he'd given her earlier when she'd wondered how he'd known her shoe size. "I guessed. Plus Italian food is what I do best."

"Whatever we're having smells wonderful."

"Lasagna," she said. "My family are all health-food nuts, and when I went away to college, I dove off the deep end when it came to food that was not good for me." She sliced a green pepper in half and scraped out the seeds. "Luckily I had a roommate with a Sicilian grandmother who had taught her how to cook, so I was weaned off junk food by pasta. By watching her I learned to make a number of dishes I can't pronounce."

At that moment the wall phone next to the

stove rang. Coral wiped her hands off on a towel and, after excusing herself, answered it.

She frowned when she heard her niece's voice. "Is everything all right, Sally?"

Paul remained where he was instead of politely stepping out of the room in case she wanted to have a private conversation. He leaned forward and snitched a slice of cucumber from the salad bowl, grinning when Coral playfully tapped his hand. He could see the advantages to a small kitchen.

A full minute went by as she listened to Sally's problem. "I'll have to check my schedule," she said at last. After a short pause she answered, 'I can't promise to be there, Sally. I've told you not to count on me for any school programs if they're during the week." Her voice changed, her tone full of regret. "I wish he would, too, honey, but your father has to deal with things in his own way. He isn't comfortable around a lot of people."

Coral heard the chime of the food timer. "I have to go, Sally. I'll call you tomorrow night and let you know if I can get away."

She hung up the receiver and picked up two oven mitts off the counter next to the stove. A few seconds later a large pan of lasagna was cooling on a rack.

Then Coral excused herself again and returned to the living room. Paul was able to see what she was doing without having to move, so

he remained where he was while she opened her
briefcase and took out a thick, well-worn organizer book. She turned to a certain section, then
she did a curious thing. She took out a clear
plastic case that appeared to hold a set of different-colored pens. Choosing one, she jotted
something down on the page in front of her;
picking another pen, she wrote something else
down.

Paul's curiosity got the better of him. "Why
are you using different-colored pens?"

She looked up. "I use various colors to de-
note certain people. When I glance at the calen-
dar page, I know who the note refers to
instantly." She held up the pink pen she'd been
writing with. "Pink is my niece, Sally, whom I
just talked to on the phone. I made a note to call
her tomorrow night."

"You used a blue pen first."

"That's to have Louise check my schedule
for Thursday to see if I can take off early in order to drive to Charlottesville by seven in the
evening."

His interest was piqued even more. "Have I
been assigned a color?"

Coral was suddenly intent on closing her organizer book and putting it and the set of pens
away neatly in her case as though she hadn't
heard the question. She returned the case to the
floor beside the desk, where she had put it when
she first arrived home.

Still not answering Paul, she walked over to the drapes that covered one side of her living room. Drawing them open, she revealed a wall of glass. She opened the sliding door leading out to a small balcony. A circular wrought-iron table sat near the railing with two matching chairs. Cushions covered in a vine-patterned material on a white background had been placed on the hard metal chairs for comfort. Several potted vines hung from hooks overhead and more plants were set around in the corners, giving the appearance of the great outdoors.

"I thought we'd eat on the balcony," she said with a wave of her hand as she walked back toward him.

He didn't bother to hide his amusement. "So what color am I?"

"Purple," she muttered as she busied herself with putting placemats, napkins, seasonings, and wineglasses on a tray.

"Why purple?"

"You're English. Purple is a royal color. It seemed right somehow."

"I'm glad you didn't choose pink for me. I have an aversion to it. Lindsay's room at Tysdale had been done in a sticky pink. Made me think of candy floss. I believe you call it cotton candy."

She handed the tray to him. "Would you set the table? While you're doing that, I'll put the garlic bread under the broiler. We'll both be done at the same time and then we'll eat all that much sooner."

He glanced at the tray. "Where do you keep your cutlery? Eating lasagna with our fingers could get messy."

Coral figured *cutlery* meant "silverware," so she indicated the drawer to the left of the sink. "You'll find everything you need in there."

Her attention was on the slices of bread she'd slipped under the broiler while he rummaged around for quite a considerable amount of time. She had taken the pan of toasted bread out when he finally headed toward the balcony with the tray.

By the time she'd placed portions of lasagna on plates and dished out salad into bowls, Paul had returned to the kitchen with an empty tray. She filled the tray again with their dinner and handed him the basket of fragrant garlic bread.

When she stepped onto the balcony, Coral immediately spotted the addition to the table that Paul had come up with on his own. He'd taken one of the wide pillar candles off her coffee table and set it in the middle of the wrought-iron table. With the sun fading over the horizon, the flickering flame reflected off the leaves of the plants and the glassware, creating a glowing intimacy that had been missing before.

He had also used just about every piece of silverware in the drawer when he'd set the table, she noticed. She counted three forks on the left, two spoons next to the knife on the right, and a larger spoon placed horizonally above where their plates would sit.

"I hope you aren't expecting a seven-course meal." She glanced down at the plates she held. "This is basically our dinner."

Paul looked at the table. "Too many forks and spoons?"

"A few. Have you ever set a table before?"

"The occasion hasn't come up until tonight. I went by the way our places are set at Tysdale." He shrugged. "Just ignore the utensils you don't plan on using."

"Is this how you usually eat?" she asked, a hint of awe in her voice as she glanced at the profusion of forks and spoons.

"I've never thought about it. I dine out or fix a sandwich or snack on crackers and cheese when I'm at my house in Georgetown. Why are you making such a big deal out of the way I set the table?"

"I'm sorry. I'm being rude. It's just that I don't want you to be disappointed in the simple dinner I've fixed if you're used to fifty courses."

He smiled. "I'm going to be vastly disappointed if I never get to eat it."

Once again, Coral dismissed the subject of their differences. But she had a feeling there would be many more incidents that pointed out the lack of similarities in their backgrounds.

The distance between the son of a British

peer and the daughter of an entomologist was farther than mere geography.

After she placed their plates on the table and arranged a spot for the basket of bread, she invited him to be seated. He had plans of his own. He walked over to her chair and pulled it away from the table, then waited for her to sit down.

She smiled at him before turning her back in order to sit down. "Your mother would be so proud."

"It's amazing how many of her admonitions stuck." Paul sat down across from her. "As far as she's concerned, there is no excuse for bad manners, no matter what a person's station in life or the circumstances. I'll probably go to my grave hearing her say that it costs nothing to be civil. She took an active role in the deportment part of our upbringing."

"There must be a universal handbook on motherhood that emphasizes that manners must be drilled into offspring, although my mother doesn't restrict her teachings to just the family. My mother would expect a burglar to apologize for making a mess."

"Your mother and mine could be cut from the same cloth. After a particularly grueling polo match, Reggie had a sprained wrist from one of several falls from his horse and had bits of sod sticking to his boots and silks. He was able to go for medical treatment only after he had said all the right things to some friends of my parents whom they had brought with them."

Coral was aware of the affection in his voice when he spoke about his mother and his brother. Being close to their families was one thing they had in common at least.

They were halfway through the meal when the phone ringing in the living room interrupted their lively discussion about Coral's schedule. Coral excused herself and went to answer it.

This time the conversation was short but not at all sweet. Coral returned to her chair and respread her napkin on her lap, her expression giving Paul the impression she had not received good news.

He reached for another slice of garlic bread. "Do you want to talk about it?"

She set her wineglass down after taking a drink. "That was the woman who usually cooks and cleans for my family. She has to have surgery on her feet and will have to rest for several weeks afterwards, so she won't be able to work. She's arranged for her sister to fill in for her during that time, which saves me from having to hire someone temporarily."

"That sounds more like a solution than a problem."

"My parents prefer a routine, especially my father. They don't take change very well."

"If the work is done, what difference does it make who actually does it?"

"None, I hope. Not everyone is tolerant of my families' various eccentricities, though." She smiled. "Some people actually take exception to moving aside a container of fireflies in order to set down a bowl of potatoes or having a small mechanical figure walk across the table or be asked to bake three cakes with varying ingredients for a taste test for my sister-in-law's latest cookbook."

"Why did the woman call you instead of notifying your parents?"

"I hired her. I pay her salary. She technically works for me. Do you want another helping of lasagna?"

He shook his head, more interested in what she was saying than what he was eating. "Why doesn't your family take care of their own arrangements for that sort of thing? I would think it would be more convenient for them to handle their own affairs there than for you to sort things out from here."

"I haven't thought much about it. It's something I've always done."

"What do you mean, 'always'?"

Coral frowned at the intensity in his voice. "What part of the word don't you understand? I mean for as long as I can remember, from the time I could help make things easier for them to do their work."

Paul liked what he was hearing less and less.

"Why do you feel it's your job to make their lives easier?"

"Because it's the one thing I can do. Supporting them is my contribution. I don't have the ability to make any scientific discoveries, but I can make it possible for them to continue their work."

"This is worse than I thought. You're supporting them financially, aren't you?"

Coral didn't like his tone, which implied she was doing something illicit. "Not entirely, but I do help out."

"I don't believe this. How many people are we talking about here? Your parents, two brothers, a sister-in-law, a niece, and a housekeeper?"

"You forgot Aaron, my nephew."

"I find it hard to accept that your family expects you to support them."

"I've told you about my parents and my brothers. They are inventors, discoverers, scholars, researchers, experts in their fields. What they do is important. They are important."

"More important than you?"

She had been in the process of sipping some wine and nearly choked when she heard his question. He leaned forward to thump her on the back several times until she caught her breath.

"Thank you," she said in a wavering voice.

"My pleasure. If there is anyone who needs to be shaken out of her routine, it's you. Just because you've always done something doesn't mean you have to do it for the rest of your life."

She stared at him. "I like routine." She sounded defensive, and she hated that. "And I like to help my family."

"I'm not implying there is anything wrong with helping your family, but your life should be more balanced. Right now it seems to me you primarily run Quality Interior Design and take care of your family. What about you? When was the last time you did something for yourself that had nothing to do with your family?"

"I went to Montego Qui's concert," she said with a hint of mutiny.

Paul didn't point out that he had been instrumental in getting her there. If he hadn't pushed her, she wouldn't have gone.

"And before that?"

Coral's brow creased as she searched her memory bank for an answer. Her frown deepened when she couldn't come up with any occasion to give him. Pushing back her chair, she stood and began gathering their dishes.

"Not everyone lives for fun and games."

"If that shot was directed toward my lifestyle, it fell short of the mark. Outfitters give a number of people a chance to relax and unwind from the pressures of work and family. In some cases we possibly even save a few of our customers from heart attacks brought on by stress by providing them with an outlet they badly need.

Tripod might not seem important up against discovering a substance to grow old seeds in, but if we save one kid from killing someone or himself, it will be worth it."

Dishes clattered noisily when she set the tray down abruptly. "I'm sorry. I didn't mean it to sound like I was belittling your choices." She sighed. "I'm more defensive about my position in my family than I thought."

"Quit apologizing." Paul stood and stepped around the table. He cupped her face in his warm hands. "My intent isn't to make you feel guilty. I want you to think about how much of your life is dedicated to your family without leaving anything for yourself. I also have to wonder where I'll fit in between family obligations and financial responsibilities."

She brought her hands up to hold his wrists. "One of the things I do best is organize things, remember? With a little planning I'm sure I can work you into my schedule."

Even though she was smiling, Paul didn't see the humor in her statement. He didn't want to be just another entry in her organizer book, his name written in purple ink so that she could distinguish him from the other demands on her time.

He slid his fingers through her hair, holding her firmly as he lowered his head. With an unexpected desperation, he kissed her deeply. His whole body responded to the enticing pleasure he found within her. The chill of fear he hadn't recognized until that moment faded with the warmth of her natural response, but it didn't disappear entirely.

Finding the other half of himself left him vulnerable to the fear of losing it.

With a soft yearning sound, Coral raised up on her toes and wrapped her arms around his neck. She was suddenly ravenous for his touch, his taste, and the rush of desire she experienced with him.

His hands explored, his arms surrounded, his mouth sweetly ravaged her lips and throat until she was almost mindless. He was generous but also demanding, and Coral shared her passion without any reservations. She felt oddly triumphant when Paul shuddered against her as she slid her hand over his hip and thigh and back to his waist where she clung to him.

Groaning, Paul broke away from her mouth and buried his face in the damp curve of her throat. His heart was racing, his lungs gasping for air as he tried to control the raging fever in his blood.

It took an incredible effort to lift his head in order to see her face. "I know this wasn't on your agenda for the evening, but don't refuse me, Coral. I want you and you want me. Let that be enough for tonight."

SEVEN

Let that be enough for tonight. Paul's words echoed in Coral's head as she looked deeply into his eyes, searching for the answer her heart and body had already given. She loved him with every ounce of her being, she understood that now. She could no more hold back that feeling than she could deny it.

He was offering her only tonight when she wanted all of his tomorrows. If this was all she was going to have, then she should think carefully before she committed herself to accepting his terms. The problem was she couldn't think rationally. Her body was vibrating with sexual tension and a desire so strong, she felt dazed.

She was unable to put her feelings into words. She didn't know the right ones that would correctly describe the riot of emotions he created within her. A smile, a touch, a word spoken in his distinct accent. The cause didn't matter. The way he made her feel did.

She heard his quick intake of breath when she turned away from him toward the table. He thought she was rejecting him, she realized. She had no way of knowing if he was surprised or disappointed. She ignored the tray of dishes and reached for the lighted candle in the center of the table. Cupping the burning wick with her free hand, she kept her gaze on the flame until she faced Paul again.

The reflection of the candlelight glimmered in his eyes when she met his dark gaze. "Would you like to bring the wine into my bedroom?"

He shook his head, passion flaring in his eyes with the knowledge that she was yielding to desire after all. "I don't think we need it, do you?"

The husky timbre of his voice added to the intimacy of the moment. Coral sounded oddly hoarse herself when she murmured, "I'm having trouble keeping a clear head as it is."

"You have no reason to believe me, Coral, but you can trust me. I'll take care of you. You won't have any reason to regret our time together."

Coral didn't want to talk about regrets. She would deal with them later. And there were bound to be more than a few.

Holding the candle in front of her, she stepped into the living room and carefully protected the flame from flickering out as she walked down the hall to her bedroom. The candlelight added a soft glow to the polished mahogany furnishings and the quilted velvet comforter spread over her four-poster bed.

She set the candle on the dresser, and the mirror behind it reflected the warm candlelight back across the room. Coral caught Paul's reflection in the mirror too. He stood in the doorway, his eyes watching her every gesture, every breath she took, every shiver of arousal she couldn't control.

With her gaze on his in the mirror, she brought her hands up and slowly pulled her vest off, letting the garment slide down her arms and onto the floor. Everything about Paul, his expression, his stiff posture, even the way he breathed, revealed his desire, and she couldn't look away from his mirrored image as she began to unfasten her shirt.

Paul walked slowly toward her, his eyes never leaving her reflection as he stopped close behind her. "I might not be sane when this is over," he said quietly.

A haunted sadness dimmed her eyes for a few seconds, then was gone before he could convince himself he'd seen such a devastated expression. He watched her intently, wondering what had caused her to look so forlorn, but he saw only the glazed heat of her feminine arousal.

Unable to be a spectator any longer, he moved forward until her back was pressed against his chest. Slipping his arms under hers, he took over unbuttoning her shirt when her fingers fumbled with the task.

Coral worried her bottom lip with her teeth. She had to fight against giving in entirely to the magic of his nearness and the warmth of his body so closely aligned with hers. But first she had to make something clear.

"Paul?"

"Hmmm?"

"I don't want you to think I do this all the time."

His nimble fingers parted the front opening of her shirt. "You don't undress often?"

She blew out a breath. Honestly, she thought with exasperation, for an intelligent man, he could be bone dumb sometimes.

"I don't go to bed with someone I've known such a short time. Or do this sort of thing at all." Her mouth twisted into a strained smile of self-mockery. "It sounds old-fashioned, but I'd like you to still respect me in the morning."

He placed his hands on her shoulders and turned her around to face him. "You have no reason to believe me, but I don't make a habit of falling into bed with every woman I have dinner with either. I can't recall ever wanting anything or anyone as badly as I want you." His gaze darkened with emotion. "I know it bothers you that it appears that we don't have a great deal in common, but we do have this."

This turned out to be her quickened breathing when he covered her breast with his hand, and his thudding heartbeat when he placed her hand in the middle of his chest.

"I thought I had experienced every thrill that existed," he said against her throat. "But with you I'm discovering I've only scratched the surface of sensations."

Coral shivered with reaction as his hand flowed over the curve of her shoulder, down her arm, across her hip and thigh. His other hand circled the nape of her neck while his mouth seduced her with moist, tantalizing kisses along her jawline, her throat, the sensitive place behind her left ear.

"Paul," she whispered achingly.

"Touch me," he groaned. "I want to feel your hands on me."

Along with all the other sensations, Coral was aware of a fierce need to give him as much pleasure as he was giving her. She had never considered herself a sensual woman. Until now. The gift of knowing that side of herself existed was a priceless one, and she wanted to share her exultation with the man who was responsible.

Her hands went to his belt, her fingers surprisingly sure and steady as she manipulated the buckle and unfastened the closure of his slacks. She gloried in the tremor that shook him when she trailed her fingers over his waist just above the fabric of his slacks.

Suddenly the room tilted as she was lifted off her feet. The mattress gave with the combined weight of their bodies as he followed her down onto the velvet spread. The barrier of their clothing became unbearable. The craving for closeness was all-consuming, and they worked together to remove the obstacles preventing them from experiencing the ultimate intimacy.

As Paul held her naked body in his arms and felt her straining to get closer, he realized Coral's business persona had been stripped away with her clothes. She was a cool professional during the day, but wild in the night.

He kissed her deeply time and time again until she was mindless with passion and his control was dangerously close to snapping. He made a hoarse sound deep in his throat when he felt her delicate fingers slide over his hip and thigh and clench his buttocks.

Knowing she wanted him gave Paul the most incredibly joyous sensation he'd ever experienced. His entire body felt tight and coiled to an impossible degree. He had to have her or explode into a million fragments.

She raised her hips to meet the pressure of his hand and she murmured his name over and over in a litany of need. She was moist and hot and hungry as she moved against his fingers.

His pulse was pounding loudly in his ears when he lifted his head and looked into her eyes.

"Nothing's going to be the same," he murmured with certainty as he lowered his hips between her legs. "You know that, don't you? Nothing this powerful can leave us unchanged."

"It's too late." She felt his hard length at the threshold of her aching body. "Wanting you has already changed me."

Paul closed his eyes briefly as a surge of desire flared through him. Then he opened them so that he could see into her soul as he slowly pushed into her. His body shuddered as he felt her close around him, nearly claiming his control as intense pleasure, urgent and explosive, washed over him.

He felt the spasmodic clenching of her body signaling her release, and he drove into her so deep and complete, he nearly lost consciousness as the world shattered around him.

It took a long time for them to surface from the depths of sensuality they'd shared. Paul finally had enough presence of mind to realize he was crushing her with his weight. Coral made a sound of protest when he eased himself from her body, and he leaned over to soothe her with a brief touch of his lips. Lying on his back, he kept one arm around her, holding her firmly against his side.

Her head was on his shoulder, her hand on his chest over his heart. Her eyes were closed, her skin glistening and damp in the candlelight. The rising and falling of her breasts gradually slowed as she came down to earth again.

He had never seen anything so emotionally stirring or so deeply rewarding as the sight of flushed satisfaction on her face, knowing he had been responsible for putting it there.

The full impact of the words he'd muttered just before he claimed her came back to him full force.

Everything had changed.

"Paul?"

Her voice was drowsy, the throaty sound arousing him when he thought such a thing would be impossible so soon after the last tumultuous minutes.

"I thought you were asleep."

"Almost. Will you stay the night?"

A flare of panic tightened his throat. Stalling, he asked, "Do you want me to?"

"Yes," she answered frankly.

Paul felt ridiculous. How could he tell her that spending the rest of the night in her bed was more of a commitment than he felt he could make? Considering the intimacy of the lovemaking they'd just shared, he would sound crazy. Maybe that was the explanation. He'd lost his mind.

He needed some time and space to think about the change in their relationship. The change inside himself.

"We both need to get up early and go to work," he said. "It would be more practical for me to leave soon so that you can get some sleep."

Even though she hadn't moved so much as an eyelash, Paul sensed her withdrawal. His sensitivity to what she was thinking and feeling was yet another indication of how different this affair was from any other.

"I understand," she murmured.

He scowled at the subdued tone of her voice, which was a clear indication she didn't understand.

At that moment the candle flame flickered several times and guttered out, leaving the bedroom in complete darkness. He had no way of seeing her expression unless he turned on one of the bedside lamps, and he hesitated to do that. Seeing her naked splendor would only make it more difficult for him to leave, and his inner turmoil might be visible in his expression. If she asked him what was wrong, he'd have no answer to give her. How could he explain his confusion to her when he couldn't explain it to himself? Until he came to terms with the jumble of emotions she had created within him, he had no right to stay when he would want her again and again.

"I'll stay until you're asleep."

"That's not necessary," she said quietly.

He was irrationally annoyed that she appeared to want to be rid of him although he was the one who'd said he should leave.

"I'll wait," he said stubbornly.

She rolled away from him onto her other side so that she was facing the wall.

He felt her tug at the velvet spread, which had slid to the foot of the bed. The rustle of fabric ceased once she had pulled the cover over her naked body. The thought that she was embarrassed to be unclothed with him in a dark room made him reconsider his plan to leave.

"Coral, if you want me to stay, I will."

"No, thank you," she murmured. "Good night, Paul."

He winced at the way her voice wavered when she said his name. The thought that he had hurt her made him almost reach out for her, until he remembered what he needed to think about. He could possibly hurt her a great deal worse if he didn't decide first how far he wanted to take their relationship.

He lay stiffly on her bed, staring at the ceiling he couldn't see, waiting until she fell asleep before he could bring himself to leave. Then he wouldn't feel as though he'd just used her for his own gratification and left as soon as he'd gotten it. He realized it was a puny rationalization, but he made it anyway.

He heard the soft ticking of the small bedside clock on his side of her bed. Five minutes passed before he became aware her breathing was deep and slow.

He made every effort to leave the bed without disturbing her. The last thing he wanted was for her to waken. He didn't know how to explain the urgency he felt to leave. The multitude of powerful emotions had crashed over him like an avalanche, burying him under their weight. While he was with her, he wouldn't be able to dig himself out from the passionate hold she had on him.

For both their sakes he needed time to think which direction he was prepared for their relationship to go. The only long-term commitment he'd ever made in his life was with John when they had formed Outfitters. Even so, he'd still been able to continue his basic lifestyle without making any major changes. John, on the other hand, no longer accompanied him on any trips. Not since he'd married his wife, Victoria. Victoria had been too afraid John would seriously hurt himself, or even get himself killed. Although John had acquiesced to his wife's demands, he had admitted to Paul once that he missed the adventures they used to have, even the dangerous ones.

Paul had decided a long time ago to refrain from the questionable joys of hearth and home and the restrictions that automatically came with them. Amazingly his severest critic, his loving sister, had agreed with him when he'd casually mentioned abstaining from marriage. To his chagrin she had strongly agreed with him, declaring that he'd been born too late. The days of women wanting a knight-errant were over. Women slayed their own bloody dragons and didn't want to see a man briefly in between crusades.

Paul had some serious thinking to do.

The sound he made when he zipped up his slacks seemed obscenely loud in the silent bedroom, but Coral's breathing didn't change. He tugged on his shirt and swept his hand around the carpet to search for his socks and shoes. When his fingers touched her silky panties, he nearly groaned aloud as his body hardened with the memory of stripping them down her legs.

And how her thighs had clasped his hips when he was so deep inside her, he felt as though they were one person.

A film of sweat coated his skin as the memories crowded out every reasonable thought. With a desperation born of a man on the edge, he intensified his search and finally found his shoes. He stood and walked toward the door without looking for his socks. A man could only take so much.

When she heard the soft click of the latch on her bedroom door, Coral opened her eyes and stared at the wall. The tightness in her chest felt as though she would be crushed by the devastation in her heart. She was beyond tears, beyond hope, and feeling more incredibly stupid than she ever had in her life.

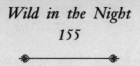

At noon on Thursday Coral picked up the phone to make her last call before she could leave the office. She dialed the number and asked to speak to Tom Grogan when his secretary answered the phone.

Louise appeared in the doorway as Coral was told that Mr. Grogan was out to lunch. Coral beckoned Louise to come into her office and instructed the secretary to tell Mr. Grogan that Coral Bentley of Quality Interior Designs had returned his call.

"He'll be unable to reach me until Monday," she went on, "at which time we can discuss the cost estimates for the acoustical partitions he's interested in installing. We have a meeting scheduled at three on Monday. In the meantime I'll fax a copy of the figures immediately so that he will have them to study."

Half a minute later Coral disconnected the call and separated a folder from the others on her desk. She stood and held out the file to Louise, who had positioned her wheelchair on the opposite side of the desk.

"The top sheet needs to be faxed to Grogan and Associates sometime this afternoon. That's the last thing on my list, so if you can't think of anything else I need to do before I leave, I'll take off."

Louise held up four pink message slips. "What about these?"

Since Louise had waited until now to give her the messages, Coral knew whose name she would find on the slips of paper. Her secretary had chosen to present the messages when Coral couldn't use the excuse of having work to do before she answered the calls.

She reached out her hand to take the messages. Leafing through them quickly, she confirmed that they were all from Paul Forge. She balled them up and flung them in the wastepaper basket beside her desk.

"You gave him Steven's extension number, didn't you?"

Louise nodded. "Each time he's phoned, just like you asked. And when I do, he tells me in that refined voice of his that he wants you."

The choice of words was unfortunate. Paul had wanted her before in a much more personal way, and like a lovesick fool she had taken him to her bed. The word *want* didn't mean the same thing to Paul that it did to her. She had wanted him forever, and he had wanted her for a couple of hours.

He could be calling her office because he couldn't find the file on alligator wrestling in the Florida Everglades, but she doubted it.

She really couldn't blame him for expecting her to repeat the evening's intimate festivities. She had fallen into bed with him with disgusting speed. She cringed every time she thought about how easily she had succumbed to the desire he aroused in her with so little effort.

"Are you okay?" Louise asked.

"Of course. Why do you ask?"

With a quick motion of her head Louise drew Coral's attention to where she'd put her hand. Without realizing it, Coral had flattened her hand on her stomach. Between weary depression, a queasy stomach, and lack of sleep, she had not been able to eat much, and her system was rebelling against the absence of food and rest.

Coral took a roll of antacids from the top drawer of her desk, peeled off a tablet, and popped it into her mouth. "I haven't taken time to eat much the last couple of days. I'll stop and get something on my way."

She was anxious to get out of the office in case Paul decided to stake his claim in person. He'd shown up the day before at four-thirty, but she'd had a meeting out of the office. When she'd called Louise on her car phone, she'd discovered he was there asking for her. She'd instructed Louise to tell him that she wouldn't be returning to the office, nor would she be home until late, just in case he decided to show up at her apartment.

She'd had dinner alone in a restaurant, which she hadn't enjoyed, and gone to a movie she didn't watch. Irritated with herself for allowing the thought of seeing Paul again to keep her from going home, she'd returned to her apartment late in the evening.

Instead of being discouraged, Paul had simply intensified his phone messages. He would come to her office again, and she couldn't blame him for expecting her to be pleased to see him. She certainly hadn't played hard to get the last time.

She handed the stack of updated files to Louise, which cleared her desk of everything but her purse and briefcase.

"How long have I worked for you, Coral?" Louise asked as Coral slung her purse strap over her shoulder.

Coral thought back to the day Louise had wheeled into her office, all aggressive spirit and cocky talent. "It will be three years next March. Why? Are you hitting me up for a raise?"

Louise shook her head. "I've had a raise this year. In all that time have I ever stepped out of bounds, pardon the pun, interfered in your personal life other than spend a few weekends with your family when you invited me?"

Coral had a sinking feeling she knew where this was leading, and she didn't want to go there. "My family is about the extent of my personal life."

"I'm worried about you, boss. I've never seen you like you've been since Tuesday. Even when the business was just crawling along at first, you never popped antacids or set a backbreaking schedule for yourself from sunup to sundown with very little breathing room in between. If your accountant had run off with the company's profits, I could understand you being in a panic about business, but that isn't the case." She glanced at the wastebasket. "I have a gut feeling our friend from the land of tea and crumpets is behind this, and my gut is seldom wrong."

"You tell your gut that I'm fine. I had a momentary lapse of sanity involving Mr. Forge, but I've come to my senses, so you don't need to worry about me." Coral stepped around her desk and put her hand on Louise's shoulder. "But I appreciate the concern. You've just reminded me that my judgment in people was certainly working well when I hired you. Recent experiences had me doubting I had any sense at all."

Louise placed her hand over Coral's. "I'm sorry things didn't work out."

Coral smiled faintly. "I am too. I'm putting this down to one of life's little jests. Maybe someday I'll even be able to laugh about it."

"Is there anything I can do?" Louise asked. "Run over his foot with my chair if he comes here again? Tell him to climb the nearest flagpole the next time he calls? Whatever you want me to do, I'll do it."

For the first time in three days Coral found she still had a sense of humor.

"Thanks anyway. These things have a habit of blowing over. If he continues calling, keep trying to hand him over to Steven or Edie if he's got a problem relating to business. If it's a personal call, feel free to direct him to the flagpole of your choosing." She reached for her briefcase. "Hold down the fort while I'm gone. I'll see you on Monday."

When she walked out of her office, Louise followed. "Did you remember to pack my present to your mother?"

Coral patted the case with her hand. "It's in here. She'll love the poem you wrote in calligraphy. I wish you could have come with me for the weekend."

"Me too. But this is the first weekend my sister has been able to get off from hospital duty. That's what she gets for being such a good emergency-room nurse." Louise held the door after Coral opened it. "We'll do each other's hair and nails, make popcorn and fudge, stuff ourselves silly, and stay up half the night talking."

"It sounds terrific."

"It will be if she doesn't start in again about another operation on my hip. Drive carefully, boss. The job you save will be mine."

The phone on Louise's desk rang.

The two women's gazes met. Coral's lips formed a rueful smile. "I'll see you on Monday."

Coral walked out the door and turned

toward the bank of elevators down the hall. Louise closed the outer office door, but Coral could swear she still heard the strident sound of the phone ringing, a sound she'd come to dread during the last couple of days.

She stepped into the elevator and disciplined her mind to think of the school program she would be attending with Sally later that evening and the surprise birthday party for her mother.

A few minutes later she left the elevator and walked across the large ground-floor lobby. She lifted her chin and straightened her spine, determined to file her recent experience with Paul under the heading of Really Stupid Stuff and get on with her life.

She suddenly stopped walking and leaned against the marble-lined wall in the lobby. Her shoulders slumped and her lips trembled. Who was she kidding? she chided herself.

The emptiness in her heart caused actual pain in her chest that no medicine could ever take away. It would be impossible to forget Paul or the passion that had drawn them together. She had only been fooling herself thinking she could.

Her instincts screamed loudly that those tumultuous moments in his arms could never be duplicated with any other man. Never again would she experience the natural feeling of being half of a whole. Being with Paul had completed her somehow, brought out the best in herself. She hadn't missed what she hadn't known existed. Until now.

How could she have been so wrong about something that felt so right? she asked herself in vain.

An overwhelming depression washed over her, making her feel remarkably old and spent for a woman only twenty-eight years old.

Love was the key that had unlocked the hot rush of desire she'd hidden away even from herself. Love was the cause of the most deliriously happy moments she'd ever experienced.

Love was the reason she was feeling more lonely than she'd ever felt in her life.

EIGHT

When Coral parked her car in her assigned spot at her apartment complex, it was after midnight, technically early Monday morning. She usually returned from the farm late Sunday afternoon, arriving back at her apartment in time for a light meal and a relaxing bath before going to bed.

The loss of sleep was well worth it when she thought of her mother's expression when she'd seen the fairy lights flickering in the trees and had watched her favorite movie under the stars with her family all around her. Everyone had done their part in preparing for the surprise, including Coral's father, who had remembered to carry out his mission of getting his wife to the glade in the woods at the appointed time.

Coral smiled to herself as she unloaded the things she'd packed in the trunk of her car onto one of the carts provided for the tenants' use.

Her mother's face had glowed with pleasure in
the lantern light as she sat holding hands with
her husband, with her children and her grand-
children nearby.

Her family might appear unorthodox in
some people's eyes, but they were the most
loyal, loving people Coral knew. Spending the
weekend with them had been a time of healing
for her after the bruising her pride had taken
from her experience with Paul. If anyone noticed she was quieter than usual, no one pestered
her with questions. Individual privacy was re-
spected and honored in her family, unless any of
them needed a shoulder to cry or lean on.

As she put her suitcase on the cart, she remembered that her brother Guthrie had given
her an unusually long hug when she was ready to
leave and had said, *"Illegitimi non carborundum.*
(Don't let the bastards get you down)."

It was as good advice as any. The elevator
was empty and silent except for the sound of the
mechanism propelling it upward. Considering it
was after midnight, she wasn't surprised no one
else was going out or coming in. Most of the
other residents in the apartment complex were
working singles and couples along with a few retired people. Hardly a party crowd.

Returning from the farm usually required a
brief period of adjustment. Her apartment always seemed so empty and quiet after the clatter
of eight people moving around in the farm-

house. Floors squeaked, radios blared, teakettles whistled, doors slammed, timers chimed, Aaron teased, Sally protested. Home sweet home.

Coral wrestled with the cart when the elevator stopped at her floor, finally managing to get the wheels over the sill and onto the carpet. Her denim skirt nearly got caught in the doors as they slid shut, but she pulled it out of the way. Luckily she didn't have to push the cart far. Her apartment was only two doors down the hall.

She had brought more stuff back than usual. The vegetable and experimental gardens were producing bountiful crops, plus her mother had made a large supply of granola, muesli, couscous, and whole-grain muffins. The largest box contained one of Guthrie's clocks, to be delivered to a jewelry store in Pentagon Mall.

She used one hand on the cart while she fished inside her vest pocket for her keys with her other hand. Since her attention was on her search and not on her surroundings, she didn't immediately notice that her neighbor across the hall had his door wide open.

Mr. Psandris was in his seventies and lived alone. He rarely left his apartment due to crippling arthritis. He often had visitors, which wasn't surprising. He was a friendly, kind man with a devilish sense of humor. Coral doubted if any of his elderly friends would be visiting this late. His son lived somewhere in the Northwest, so Coral doubted he would be the reason the door was open.

Leaving the cart near her own door, she walked over to the elderly man's apartment. "Mr. Psandris? Are you home?"

She heard the older man's deep chuckle. "Of course. Where else would I be?"

"Why is your door open?" she asked as she stepped into the small foyer. "Are you all right?"

"I've never been better."

Coral wanted to see for herself. His apartment was designed exactly like hers except in reverse. From there the similarity ended. The living room was in tans and browns with a sprinkling of lime green and was packed with furniture he had hated to get rid of when he'd moved from a large house into the small apartment after his wife died.

A rotund man who shared her penchant for vests, he wore his standard attire of shirt and tie along with a red-and-black-checkered vest and black slacks. He resembled a jolly Saint Nick, though he sported a fine white, bushy mustache instead of a beard. Tufts of white hair sprang from the sides of his head just above his ears like wisps of cotton.

From the depths of his recliner he said, "Come in, Coral. Come in and sit down. You must be tired after your drive from Charlottesville."

She walked over to his chair only to reassure

herself he was all right. "I can't stay but a minute. I have the usual assortment of things to take care of that I brought back from the farm. Mother sent a supply of muesli for you."

"How kind of her. Surely you can take a few minutes to catch your breath after your trip."

"Another time, Mr. Psandris. I have quite a lot to do tonight that I won't have time to do tomorrow."

"You work much too hard. What you need is someone to take you away from all your labors." His eyes behind his glasses gleamed. "Like Cinderella, you need a Prince Charming. I might be able to supply one for you this evening."

"Are you into magic, Mr. Psandris?" she asked with amusement. "You'll have your work cut out for you to produce Prince Charming. The mold was broken a long time ago."

"Do you think so? Well, let me try. One never knows what one can do until they try." He cleared his throat and raised his voice. "Oh, Prince Charming! Cinderella has arrived."

When the elderly man turned his gaze in the direction of the kitchen, Coral did too. From where she was standing, she could only see the stove. To her amazement she heard the sound of a liquid being poured, then smelled the scent of chocolate in the air. There really was someone with Mr. Psandris.

"About damn time," a male voice announced. "I'll be there in a second as soon as I get another cup."

Coral slowly brought her gaze back to her neighbor, who was thoroughly enjoying his surprise. He was grinning from ear to ear.

"What is Paul Forge doing here?" she asked.

"He's making hot chocolate," Mr. Psandris answered. "It's the darnedest thing. He's English, you know, yet he doesn't like tea. Can you imagine?"

"Shocking," she murmured.

"It's much too late in the evening for coffee, so we agreed that hot chocolate would do quite well."

She knew Paul could easily hear every word they were saying, and frankly she didn't care. "I meant, what is he doing here in your apartment?"

"Waiting for you of course. We left the door open so that we would hear you when you returned. The poor boy was leaning against the wall awaiting your arrival. Luckily I opened my door to fetch the newspaper dear Mrs. Spencer leaves for me after she reads it, and there he was. I suggested he wait for you here. You're later than usual. Paul was beginning to worry, but I told him about your mother's birthday celebration. The weather cooperated with the festivities, I trust?"

"The evening was perfect. She loved the box of chocolate-covered cherries you gave her."

"It was my pleasure."

At that moment Paul came around the corner carrying a tray. Against her better judgment, Coral looked at him, then wished she hadn't.

He was dressed casually in a pair of wellworn denim jeans and a blue plaid shirt, the long sleeves rolled up several turns. His jaw was shadowed with the need for a shave, his dark hair slightly disheveled. He looked wonderful.

He was concentrating on not spilling the cups of hot chocolate, which he had filled to the brim, but that didn't stop him from talking. "I was about to set off to see if you were in a ditch somewhere. Now that you're finally here, have some hot chocolate."

Just looking at him made her ache, so she turned away. "No, thanks. I have things to do. Do you want your door left open, Mr. Psandris, or should I close it when I leave?"

The elderly man looked puzzled. He glanced at Paul, who had set down the tray and was watching her, then at Coral and back to Paul. "I suppose you might as well close it now that we know you're home."

As she walked toward the door, she heard Paul say, "I appreciate your hospitality, Mr. Psandris. It looks like I won't be sharing the hot chocolate. Maybe another time."

"I don't know when I've enjoyed an evening more. But you'd better move quickly, lad, or you'll be locked out and have the rest of the night to finish your hot chocolate in the company of an old man rather than in the arms of a charming woman."

Paul smiled at the kindly gentleman and took his advice. His long strides caught up with Coral as she was trying to hold the door to her apartment open and push a heavily laden cart over the threshold.

He put his hand on the middle of the door to prop it open.

"I can manage," she said politely as though he were a stranger who had stopped to offer his assistance.

"Let me help."

"I'd rather do it myself." The cart was over the threshold and so was she. She put her hand on the edge of the door. "Good night, Paul."

He frowned when he heard the dismissal in her voice. The words were the same ones he'd heard the other night. He had expected anger and deserved it from her. He wasn't prepared for her cold reserve.

"I'm not going anywhere, Coral. We need to talk."

"No, we don't. I'm sorry if I gave you the wrong impression the other night. I did mention that I don't make a habit of hopping into bed with men." Her mouth twisted in self-mockery. "Under the circumstances I can see why you wouldn't believe me, but it's true."

Fear wasn't an emotion Paul felt often, but

he recognized it for what it was, and it was clawing through his insides with sharp talons. He had hurt her more than he thought, he realized. Now he was paying for his insensitivity and selfishness.

He pushed the cart to one side and stepped inside. "I'm not leaving until I've had a chance to explain my behavior the other night."

Because he was looking at her so intently, he saw the pain in her eyes before she lowered her lashes. His chest tightened with regret.

"It's late, Paul. I'm tired, and I wouldn't be good company, especially if you expected me to go to bed with you again."

That remark made him angry. He removed her hand from the door so that he could close it behind him. "The only thing I expect from you is a chance to tell you why I was such a bastard the other night."

"Some things come naturally," she said quellingly. "But I'll let you off the hook you've apparently hung yourself on. You didn't force yourself on me. I was willing to go to bed with you. I've put the whole evening down to experience and let it go at that. I suggest you do the same."

"I can't, because it was more than a one-night stand. It was a beginning. I just didn't see it that way then."

"I'm only thankful you didn't leave money on the dresser before you left," she said flatly.

"Dammit, Coral!" His voice hardened. "Don't cheapen what happened between us."

"You've already done that."

"If you try to open that door one more time, I'm going to nail it shut."

"You wouldn't dare."

"Don't bet on it, darling. A desperate man will go to surprising lengths to save something he considers necessary for his sanity."

Coral studied him for a long moment. She had seen amusement and desire in his expressive eyes, but this was the first time she'd ever witnessed his brand of steely determination.

With a heavy sigh of resignation she said, "Say what you've come to say, then."

"I think we can do better than standing in the foyer." He took her arm and led her into the living room. "Sit down, Coral." When she gave him a mutinous look, he added, "Or stand. It doesn't matter as long as you listen."

Coral sat. Folding her arms across her chest, she crossed one leg over the other. "I'm all ears."

"You're not," he said with a trace of humor. "You're stubborn, desirable, smart, and too damn organized, but definitely not all ears."

"I didn't mean that literally. I meant I'm listening, so could you please get this over with."

Instead of sitting on the sofa beside her, Paul pushed aside a large book and sat down on the coffee table. He placed his knees on either side of her legs, effectively boxing her in, and took her cold hands in his warm grasp.

"That's basically what we need to talk about," he said. "What we have isn't over. I'll do whatever I have to do to make you believe that."

Coral wished he wasn't holding her hands. She had been just fine until he touched her. Heat radiated up her arm, reminding her of how cold she'd felt when he'd left her, as though the fires of hell were chasing him.

Before he'd arrived that night, she'd been preoccupied with putting him and the time they shared out of her mind altogether. That plan hadn't been working. Now he was giving her a chance to find out what really happened that night. For her own peace of mind she needed to know.

"What did I do wrong the other night?" She looked down at their joined hands rather than meet his penetrating gaze. "I've heard that men like certain things, and I'm not very experienced. I did warn you about that." Her lips twisted into a grimace. "I haven't been able to figure out what I did or didn't do to drive you away."

If Coral had hauled off and slugged him, Paul couldn't have been more astonished. "Bloody hell, Coral. You didn't do anything wrong. It was me. You made me feel things I'd never felt before." He released one of her hands and ran his fingers through his hair. "Getting away from you so that I could think clearly about us was necessary. When I'm with you, my mind focuses only on how good you feel."

"And what conclusions did you come to when you had a chance to think?"

He studied her expression, which was curiously blank and unrevealing. He got the impression she didn't believe a word he was saying.

"The main conclusion I arrived at was that I should never have left that night. Whatever happens between us is something we both have to decide, not just me." Suddenly restless, he released her other hand and stood. He took several steps away from the sofa, then turned to face her. "There is one thing that I had to come to terms with on my own, and that was whether or not I was willing to change my lifestyle for you."

She drew her knees up and wrapped her arms around them as if she were cold. "Why would you have to change your lifestyle if you became involved with me?"

"Not if," he said firmly. "When."

"You didn't answer my question. What part of your life would you feel would have to change because of me?"

Paul felt he had ventured into dangerous territory and had better watch where he was going. He was on shaky ground as it was.

"The trips to potential holiday spots would be out."

"Why?"

He gave her a look of complete exasperation.

"I know how it works, Coral. Women think differently about some of the activities Outfitters recommends. There's an element of danger involved in a few of them, but that's what makes them a challenge."

"And that's why you like doing them. I still don't see what your business activities have to do with me."

"John used to travel almost as much as I do when we first started the company. When he met Victoria, his wife, he started turning all the trips over to me. Victoria didn't like him being gone for even a few days and objected to any type of activity that could be remotely dangerous. From her point of view they all were, even jogging."

Coral unwrapped her arms, straightened her legs, and stood. She started counting to ten, slowly and carefully, as she walked to where Paul stood.

He scowled. "Your lips are moving but nothing is coming out."

"I'm counting," she snapped. "Seven, eight, nine, ten," she finished aloud. "It didn't help." His blank expression was comical, and if she weren't so darn mad, she might have seen the humor in it. "I'm still angry."

"I know my explanation sounds pathetic, but it's unfortunately the truth."

"That's not why I'm mad." She poked him in the chest. "Don't you ever compare me with another woman in any way, shape, form, talent, or looks. I have my own opinions, my own thoughts, and my own standards. I've had to take comparisons between me and my family from strangers. I won't accept them from you." She poked him again for emphasis. "If you want to know how I feel about something, you ask me."

Paul took her hand before she could stab him with her finger a third time. The knot of tension in his gut loosened a little. He felt like a man who had gotten a reprieve from a sentence worse than death, but he still hadn't received clemency.

"I want to know how you feel about forgiving me and giving me another chance."

Coral's anger had sustained her from the moment she'd seen Paul in her neighbor's apartment, but now it was spent, replaced by a hope for something she'd thought she'd lost forever. A remnant of the sorrow she'd felt when he'd left after they'd made love still lingered, causing her throat to tighten. She hadn't realized she'd held the grief inside along with the anger. Now it overwhelmed her.

She stared at one of the buttons on his shirt while she tried to gather her tattered emotions together before attempting something major like speaking.

Paul couldn't wait. He cupped her face with his hands. "Look at me, Coral. Look at me and tell me you'll give me another chance to prove to you that I can act like a responsible grown-up and treat you like one too."

She managed to obey one of his requests. She lifted her lashes and met his gaze. Her breath hitched in her throat when she saw the tender expression on his face. Tears blurred her vision as she looked at him, and she heard him groan when a drop of moisture spilled over and trailed down her cheek.

"Oh, Lord, Coral. Don't do that! I feel like a big enough heel as it is without knowing I've made you cry."

She continued looking at him, and the tears continued to fall.

Paul took her in his arms and held her firmly, a deep anguish rising from the region of his heart. He could feel the dampness of her tears against his throat and swallowed with difficulty. The extent of her pain was humbling and made him regret his impulsive withdrawal even more.

The one comfort he had was that she wouldn't be so devastated if she didn't care about him.

He slipped his arm under her knees and lifted her off her feet. She stiffened when she realized he was entering her bedroom, but he didn't stop. He wanted to erase the bad memories and replace them with good ones. The only way he could think to do that was to return to the scene of his crime.

Between her tears and panic Coral's protest came out more garbled than coherent. The one word he did understand was *no*.

"I'm just going to hold you for a while, darling." He laid her down on the velvet spread and joined her immediately, taking her back into his arms. "I won't leave this time."

The room was dark except for a remnant of light from the lamp in the living room. It was enough for Paul to see her face. Her lashes were damp and her eyes were closed, and he couldn't tell at all what she was thinking or feeling.

"Did you know I was afraid of the dark when I was a child?" he asked softly.

She shook her head but didn't speak.

"My mother allowed me to keep the drapes open at night even though the room was cold and drafty most of the time. Otherwise it would be pitch-black, and I wouldn't be able to sleep. The windows in my room had leaded panes, the top rows made over a century ago by a local glass blower. The rest had been replaced, since it was almost impossible to see through the hand-blown glass. Branches of a large oak tree would scrape against the window and catch on the lead surrounding the panes of glass. Sometimes the moon would shine through the distorted panes and the tree and create odd images on the wall. I would lie under the covers and quiver and shake as monsters danced on the wall. I think I was about four at the time."

As he spoke, Coral's body became more pliant and relaxed in his arms. "One stormy night Reggie came into my room and found me cowering beneath the covers. He sat down on the edge of the bed to tell me I was being foolish and silly—with all the wisdom and authority of a six-year-old. There were no monsters, he assured me. Nothing was going to come and get me. Then he heard the tree branches scratch the window like fingernails on a blackboard."

He felt Coral shudder, and smiled. "Reggie also saw the shadows on the wall and was impressed enough to close the drapes."

"But you were afraid of the dark."

The indignation in her voice made him smile. "Reggie solved that problem by getting his Manchester United team lamp that was shaped like a football. You'd call it a soccer ball. It was a black-and-white ball with a ceramic scarf in the team colors wrapped around the base. My mother considered it frightfully ugly, but I thought it was quite beautiful when he flicked the switch and light shown through the white parts of the ball. I still have it."

"But not because you're still afraid of the dark."

With a ghost of a laugh he said, "I outgrew that particular childhood malady by the time I was six."

Coral shifted her position. Propping herself up on an elbow, she looked down at him. "Why did you want me to know you were once afraid of the dark?"

Lifting his hand, he slid his fingers through her hair, enjoying the feel of the silky strands gliding over his skin. His voice was serious, husky with emotion.

"I'm only human, Coral. I'm not perfect by any stretch of the imagination. Sometimes I make stupid mistakes the same as the next guy. I care what you think of me because I care about you. I can't promise I won't hurt you sometime in the future if I do something dumb, but I will promise to try not to ever make you cry again." His fingers tightened in her hair. "Give me another chance, darling. I want you in my life, just you, exclusively."

Coral leaned over and kissed him. His lips parted and his tongue surged between her teeth, instantly changing the light caress into a seductive claim. Paul rolled onto his back, his hands holding her hips to his on top of his rigid body. His mouth relentlessly moved under hers, caressing, fierce, and passionate, communicating to her the extent of his need for her.

"Touch me," he said roughly. "It feels so good when you touch me. Like warm silk. Yes," he sighed. "Like that."

Giving him pleasure only added to her own. She unbuttoned his shirt and swept her hands over his chest, her fingers greedy to feel how his hard muscles clenched wherever she stroked.

"Paul," she breathed achingly when he covered her breasts with his hands. The clasping, languorous motions of his fingers sent molten heat through her veins.

"I know," he rasped. "You're like a fever in my blood."

His hands left her breasts and moved down to her skirt. Clenching handfuls of the denim material, he finally found her bare legs underneath. His palms smoothed over the backs of her thighs until he reached the barrier of her panties. The sound she made deep in her throat when he slid several fingers under the elastic nearly made him lose what little control he had left.

"Coral," he moaned as his fingers found her moist heat. With a single movement he swept her panties down her legs. Her name was murmured against her mouth as he slid his hand between her legs and covered her with his whole hand.

His plea echoed in her ears along with the thudding of her quickened heartbeat. She moved her hands down his rib cage to the fastening of his jeans. She was aware he was holding his breath as she lowered the zipper. He let it out in a low moan of pleasure when she took him in her hand.

"That feels incredible," he said hoarsely.

Coral felt as though she were a coiled spring in danger of snapping at any moment. Unable to wait any longer, she pushed on his chest until she was upright. Lifting her hips, she took him inside her.

For a flickering second she wondered if this was the only closeness they would ever share. Then he moved against her and she couldn't think at all.

NINE

Coral woke slowly several hours later. A languid contentment seemed to have taken over her body that made her feel lazy and relaxed in a way she hadn't been in a very long time. If ever.

She stretched her arms and slid her legs over the smooth sheet under her, wallowing in a satisfaction that came as close to feeling smug as she had ever felt.

When her hand swept across the space beside her and found it empty, her joy in the morning dimmed. She opened her eyes and turned her head. The indentation in the other pillow was proof that she hadn't dreamed that Paul had been with her. The covers had been thrust back. He was gone.

She closed her eyes and bit her lip. *Oh, Lord*, she thought. *Not again.*

Then she heard the sound of the shower

running in her bathroom and realized she hadn't been abandoned for the second time after all.

She pushed aside the unpleasant memories of the recent past and concentrated on the exciting present. Which consisted of a naked man in her shower, she thought with a smile. The ideas that particular scenario conjured up were intriguing but not very practical. Real life, in the shape of her business responsibilities, had to be dealt with.

When she heard the water stop, she debated staying where she was until Paul came out of the bathroom. The temptation to start the day the way the previous one had ended was unbelievably strong, but so was her sense of duty. A number of people relied on her for their livelihood, and she had her own family to consider as well.

She smiled at the shameless hussy she'd become and was unable to dredge up even an ounce of regret. Paul had shown her she was a sensual being, capable of receiving and giving pleasure in the most basic way known to men and women.

Whatever happened between them, she would always be grateful for that knowledge.

She would never have imagined her life could change so dramatically and quickly as it had since Lord Paul Edward Tysdale Denton-Forge—he had told her his full name sometime during the night—had come into her life.

She tossed aside the covers and felt the cool air on her heated skin. It wouldn't have taken much persuasion to convince her she should hop back into bed. Especially if she wasn't alone, she thought wickedly. Yes, she had become a brazen wench.

She hurried over to her closet and took her robe off the hanger.

"If you're wearing that on my account, you needn't bother."

She turned her head and looked over her shoulder as she finished tying the belt of the robe. Paul had wrapped one of her dark purple towels around his hips. His hair was damp and had been combed only by his fingers. The shadow of a beard was gone, which meant he must have helped himself to the razor she kept in the medicine cabinet.

His smile was warm and intimate as he looked at her.

She walked over to him and raised up on her toes to kiss him. "The robe is for me. I'm cold."

He kissed her back. "You're not, you know. I can personally attest to that fact."

She lifted her arms to encircle his neck. "One of the first things I thought about this morning was that I have become completely shameless where you're concerned."

"I'm not complaining," he said with a crooked smile. "What was the second thing you thought about?"

She frowned. "About the fact I had better get out of bed instead of waiting for you to join me. I have a full day of appointments."

He'd wrapped his arms loosely around her and joined his hands just below her waist. "I do too." He chuckled at the expression of surprise on her face. "I do work, darling. As it happens, I have a lunch meeting with the owner of a chain of athletic-supply stores who might donate some equipment to Tripod if we agree to advertise his products in England. The reason I'm telling you this is so you don't get all stroppy when I fail to ask you to meet me for lunch."

She grinned. "Stroppy?"

"Browned off, loopy, mad as a March hare, go round the bend."

"I'm learning a whole new language from you."

"Among other things," he murmured.

"That too." She brought her arms back down to his chest. "As much as I'm enjoying the English lesson, the clock is ticking away. Since you aren't fond of tea, how do you feel about coffee?"

"Addicted." He bent his head to touch the spot below her ear that he knew was vulnerable to the slightest caress. "But not as much as I crave this."

Coral moaned softly and tipped her head back to give him access to her equally sensitive neck. She spread her hands across his chest, smiling with pleasure when he made a sound deep in his throat as she dragged a fingernail lightly over a male nipple.

"We're going to be late for work, aren't we?" she whispered against his throat.

His hands went to the belt of her robe. "I might just make the luncheon meeting."

Quality Interior Designs was the only thing that kept Coral's feet firmly on the ground the rest of the week. At least during the day. Every evening she felt as though she was suspended on a glorious cloud of laughter, warm companionship, and lovemaking, either in her apartment or at Paul's Georgetown townhouse.

Neither Paul nor Coral suggested they go out to a restaurant or to the theater or the cinema, as Paul referred to movies. They were with other people all day. The nights were theirs. They ate, talked, teased, and slept, eventually, together.

Paul learned that Coral's preference for wearing vests was from the time she was a slightly overweight teenager. By the time nature, maturity, and a strict abstinence from chocolate bars took care of the excess pounds, Coral had become fond of vests and found them useful and versatile.

Coral learned that as far as Paul was concerned, a kitchen was where the electric kettle was kept to heat water for instant coffee. Anything else was completely out of his league. She also discovered he had absolutely no desire to be educated in the cooking department. He survived on microwavable meat pies, Cornish pasties, cheese with crackers, and stacks of assorted meats between slices of bread that would have made the Earl of Sandwich proud.

She had hoped Paul had forgotten his idea to start her on an exercise program, but she should have known better. At least he didn't ask her to do anything more than sit-ups and stretching movements to begin with. The jogging would come later, he told her, once she'd built up her stamina.

Considering how physically active she'd been lately, she thought she was doing pretty well in the stamina department.

On Thursday she met Paul for lunch, along with his partner, John, and John's wife. Victoria didn't hesitate to tell Coral of the dangerous life John had lived until she put her size-five shoe down and forbade him from taking part in any adventures whatsoever.

After what seemed like hours but was actually only forty-five minutes, Coral used her business as an excuse to leave the table. No wonder Paul had had second thoughts about a relationship, she thought, when he'd seen how a woman had changed his partner's life.

She couldn't help thinking, though, that

John had to take some of the blame for his own unhappiness, since he allowed his wife to dictate his life. Paul wasn't like John, nor was she even close to resembling Victoria. The Keatses had to work out their problems. She and Paul had enough of their own adjustments to make.

One of the stumbling blocks she thought might eventually get in the way was her family's dependency on her. Paul was aware of a few phone calls from various members of her family at one time or another, and knew that they depended on her to take care of certain things for them. And she let them. It was up to her to change that.

The nights she stayed in his townhouse she used call forwarding to have any calls from her family transferred in case they needed to get in touch with her. Paul had no objections when she consulted him before making the arrangements.

She had yet to mention the fact that she was expected to spend the weekend at the farm. Things were going so well between her and Paul, she didn't want to bring up the subject until it was necessary.

By Friday morning she realized she had run out of time. While she was in the shower at Paul's townhouse, she decided to mention the upcoming weekend and invite him to come to the farm with her. She'd never brought a man with her before, so it would cause quite a stir with her family. She could just imagine the questions her mother would ask.

She and Paul had fallen into a morning routine quickly and easily. After the exercise ritual Paul would shower first, dress, make coffee, and read the morning newspaper while she showered and dressed. Occasionally there were spontaneous deviations from their schedules when desire was stronger than punctuality, but Coral was a willing participant.

She wasn't *that* much of a stickler for an organized existence.

When she walked into the kitchen Friday morning, she was all primed to discuss both of them driving to Charlottesville that afternoon. She sat across the table from him and took a restoring sip of the coffee he had poured for her.

She knew if she lived to be a hundred, she would never tire of looking at him. That morning he wore a crisp white shirt with tiny olive stripes in it, which matched the color of his solid silk tie. He was conservative in his choice of clothing, but eclectic in the furnishings in his townhouse. Signs of his visits to other places and countries were in every room, from a Flemish porcelain vase to a Japanese river-stone paperweight. Beautiful examples of Tysdale pottery could be found in almost every room.

Paul folded the paper and Coral set down her cup of coffee at the same time. They looked at each other with somber expressions and said the exact identical words in unison.

"I've been thinking . . ."

Paul chuckled. "Ladies first."

Not to be outdone in the manners department, Coral replied, "Age before beauty."

He shook his head and gestured for her to say what she wanted to say. Coral responded by indicating he should speak before she did.

Paul finally took the initiative. "I thought this weekend would be a good time to move the rest of your things over here."

"What?"

"There isn't a single word in that sentence that you couldn't understand. Just in case, I'll say it a different way. I want you to move in with me."

Stunned, Coral sat back in her chair. "I should have gone first after all."

Paul had expected her to be a little more enthusiastic about the prospect of living with him. "We spend most of our time here, my place being closer to our respective businesses, and there's more space in the townhouse than in your apartment."

Coral continued to stare at him without uttering a word.

He reached across the table and covered her hand with his. "I've discovered I like having you here when I walk in the door, or knowing that you'll be here soon if I get home first. I enjoy sipping a glass of wine while you instruct me on the fine art of cooking, instructions that I ignore, and while you ask me about my day and tell me about yours. I'm not sure I can ever go to sleep again without you beside me in my bed. I would even miss the fact that you, Miss Neat-and-Tidy, don't put the cap back on the toothpaste."

Coral wondered if he realized there was a word for the type of lifestyle he had just described, and it wasn't an affair. An affair stood for an association based on sex, which was an active part of their relationship, but he had just mentioned a great deal more.

The word was *marriage*.

"Don't you think we should discuss this first?" she asked.

"That's what we're doing. I state my opinion. You give me yours. We argue and debate the issue. Then we move your stuff over here."

She shook her head in bemusement. "You are so bloody arrogant."

He chuckled at her use of one of his English curse words. "If that's your side of the argument, it doesn't have much to recommend it."

Coral decided if she was going out on a limb, she had better start climbing by taking the first step. "Paul, I have plans for the weekend that were made before we became involved."

His dark eyes blazed. "Dammit, Coral, how

can you even consider being with someone else after the last few days?"

"I told you. I made the plans before we became involved."

"You can unmake them." He pushed his chair back and stood. "The fact that you haven't brought this up until now means I'm not included. How am I supposed to feel about that?"

"That's up to you."

Crossing his arms over his chest, he leaned a hip against the counter. "If it's up to me whether you go through with these plans or not, guess what my answer is?"

The stronger his voice became, the softer she spoke. She'd found it was an effective way of countering his more aggressive nature.

"Paul," she began gently, "my family is expecting me to arrive this evening and stay for the weekend. I'd like you to come with me. It's up to you whether you want to accompany me."

He became very still. "Your family?"

She nodded. "I've told you about them. There are my parents, Dennis and Ruth Bentley; my brother Guthrie and his wife, Nadine; my brother Harry and his two children, Aaron and Sally."

"Didn't you go see them last weekend?"

"I go every weekend."

"And you want me to come with you this time?"

"Yes, but I should warn you, it won't exactly

be a weekend at Disneyland. I can't guarantee that my father won't immediately go into a major dissertation on whether or not insects are color-blind and expect you to have an opinion one way or the other, or that my mother won't whisk you off to the chicken coop to help her gather eggs. What I'm trying to say is, I'll understand if you don't want to go with me."

He tilted his head to one side and studied her carefully. "It sounds like you're trying to talk me out of going."

"I thought it was only fair to warn you what you'd be getting into. You come from a completely different background than mine."

She stopped when he scowled at her. "If you bring up my title again, I'll only get mad."

"I'm not talking about a castle versus a farmhouse. It's not the place that takes getting used to. It's the people."

"I wasn't raised in a castle. It was once an abbey."

"Excuse me all to pieces," she said dryly. "I'm trying to explain that my family is considered to be on the eccentric side." She smiled faintly. "I should be telling you not to go. Once you eat natural foods all weekend, get stung by bees when my father shows off his hives, and bump your head in the attic room with the slanted roof, which is where you'll sleep, you might have second thoughts about me moving in with you."

"Why the attic? Is that some kind of endurance test for prospective suitors?"

"Not that I know of. Not mine anyway. I've never brought a man to the farm before."

Paul suddenly looked extremely pleased. "So why would I be sent to the attic?"

"The other rooms are taken. A bed was temporarily set up for Louise on the front porch because of wheelchair access, but being a healthy, strapping male, you'll get to climb two flights of stairs and try to sleep under the eaves. By yourself, I might add. I'll be alone in my room. My parents are old-fashioned in those respects."

"How do you know that if you've never brought a man home before?"

"A daughter knows her parents' feelings about her participation in the sexual arena, which in my case means none until marriage. Besides, neither Guthrie nor Harry were allowed to go past the second floor before they married the women they brought home." She grinned. "Two nights of the attic and you'll regret agreeing to go."

He shook his head as he pulled her out of her chair. "I'm the one who likes adventure, remember? If I can jump out of an airplane to go fishing in Alaska and ride whitewater rapids in a rubber raft, I can survive a weekend of twigs and honey." He ran his hands down her back to her hips. "The difficult part of the weekend will be having to sleep without your hand searching for mine in the middle of the night when you're sound asleep, or having to do without the feel of your small warm feet tangled with mine."

Her eyes widened in surprise. She didn't know she held his hand during the night. Even unconscious she didn't want to let go of him.

"I usually try to beat the rush-hour traffic." She leaned her head to one side as he nuzzled her neck. "Can you be ready to leave by three?"

He lifted her into his arms. His voice had taken on a familiar husky tone, his eyes dark with intent. "I'm ready right now. I'll need something to hold me over during the weekend fast."

Coral didn't have a single objection. The weekend was going to be a long one for her, too, now that she had experienced the joy of spending her days and nights with Paul. Like a greedy child she didn't want to share her free time or herself with anyone else but him.

She came close to telling Paul that she would put off going home that weekend, but he laid her on his bed and proceeded to take her mind off everything else but him.

Paul was ready to leave by three that afternoon, but not to accompany her to the farm for the weekend.

Coral was clearing off her desk a few minutes before she expected him to arrive when he came charging through her doorway. His expression reminded her of the first time he'd burst into her office to complain about the work they'd done for Outfitters.

Yet there was something different in his solemn expression and in the stiff way he held himself, as though prepared for a blow. She felt an ice-cold sliver of fear when she saw the pain in his eyes.

She stopped what she was doing and came around the desk to meet him, her instincts telling her something was terribly wrong. Placing her hand on his arm, she felt the tension in the corded muscles under her fingers.

"Paul? What's happened?"

"I won't be going with you this weekend after all. I have to fly to Switzerland right away. I was able to get a flight out that leaves in an hour."

Coral didn't ask why. "Do you want me to drive you to the airport?"

He shook his head. "John's waiting downstairs. He's going with me. Victoria isn't happy with either one of us, but for once he's not letting that matter. I wanted to tell you about the change of plans in person rather than making a cold phone call after I was supposed to pick you up."

Coral winced inwardly at the realization that he still wasn't sure of her. Their relationship was still too new and untried for them to know the other's reactions about situations that hadn't come up yet.

He touched her cheek with the back of his finger. "You aren't angry?"

"I asked you once before not to compare me to Victoria or anyone else. You obviously have an important reason to go to Switzerland at this time. Will you tell me why?"

"It's Reggie," he said, anguish darkening his eyes. "He was skiing when an avalanche caught him and two of his friends. I just got the call from the rescue-team captain, who knows me and knows Reggie is my brother. John and I are joining them while they search for him and the others."

Her heart clenched with fear, but she controlled it. "What can I do?"

His hand clasped hers tightly. "I called my parents in France to notify them about Reggie's accident. They're going to Tysdale Abbey to wait there. Lindsay and Taylor are heading to the Abbey too."

"You'll find your brother, and he will be alive. You have to believe that."

"I'm trying. Neither my mother nor my sister will cope with this very well and they'll be devastated if the news is bad. Will you go to Tysdale in my place and do whatever you can to keep them from falling apart? I know it's a lot to ask, but I'll be able to concentrate on what I'm doing if I know you're there taking care of them. They'll worry even more when they find out I'm going to the mountains to look for Reggie. Will you go?"

She nodded abruptly. "Of course I'll go." She took his arm and drew him toward the door of her office. "You go with John to the airport. Do whatever you have to do."

"How upset are your parents going to be when you don't go home this weekend?"

"They'll understand when I tell them why."

Paul stopped suddenly and pulled her into his arms. He held her so tightly, she found it difficult to breathe, but that didn't matter. She held him with all of her strength, giving him whatever silent comfort she could.

"He has to be all right, Coral," Paul said roughly. "He has to be."

She raised her head and touched his face. "Go find him, Paul, and bring him back. I'll take care of your family."

"Are you sure you can manage? My mother will be quite distraught, and Lindsay won't be much help."

"I'm an expert at dealing with chaos, remember?" she said, hoping she sounded more confident than she felt. "Don't worry about anything but finding your brother."

Louise looked up from her computer when Coral and Paul came out of the office. For once she had nothing to say. Since the door had been left open, the secretary had heard enough to know this was not a time for sassy remarks.

"Louise," Coral said, "call the airlines and get me a seat on the first available flight to Heathrow."

Louise picked up the phone while she thumbed open the phone book to the airlines section.

Paul tried to smile at Coral, but the effort didn't quite come off. "I wasn't sure you'd give up your weekend with your parents for me."

"I know," she said. "It's one of the things we'll talk about when you get back from Switzerland."

He gave her a blank look. "What are the others?"

"Not now. We both have things to do. The important thing now is that you get on that plane so that you can go find your brother." She slid her arms around his neck. "You be careful. If you fall down a crevasse and I never see you again, I'll personally go to your office and clean it from top to bottom."

This time his smile was genuine. He bent down to kiss her, taking his time. When he lifted his head, he looked deep into her eyes. "I'll call you at Tysdale when I know something."

She opened the door and gently shoved him into the hallway. She watched as he walked swiftly down the hall to the elevator that someone was holding for him. Just before he stepped in, he turned to look at her and lifted his hand.

Coral found it extremely difficult to keep her own hand from shaking as she waved to him. Then he stepped in and the doors closed. She wondered if this was the last time she would see him.

Turning back to the reception area, she sank down into a chair and grabbed her middle. She rocked back and forth, bent over at the waist. Fear for Paul's safety made her feel nauseous as all the hazards he could run into on the mountain slopes bombarded her brain. And how dreadful it would be for Paul and his family if Reggie couldn't be recovered alive.

Her terror for Paul and his brother was so all-consuming, she didn't realize that Louise had come over to her until the other woman placed her hand on Coral's shoulder.

"Your flight leaves in three hours," Louise said. "I took your passport out of the safe and arranged for a car to pick you up at your apartment to take you to the airport."

Coral took a deep breath and leaned back. She glanced toward her open office door, then met Louise's concerned gaze. "Did you hear what happened?"

Louise shook her head. "Not all of it. Enough to know it's serious."

"His brother and two friends were caught in an avalanche in Switzerland. Paul's going to help the rescue team look for them. He asked me to go to England to help his family through this."

"I'll hand over the estimates scheduled for next week to Steven or handle them myself. I'll postpone the appointments who only want to see you." She handed a slip of paper to Coral. "I found Tysdale Abbey on a map of the British Isles and wrote down the directions. It's about thirty miles northeast of London, and the phone number is written below. I won't call you unless there is an emergency."

"Thanks. I have one more favor to ask."

"So ask."

"There's a list of things my family wanted me to do for them. I'll phone them and explain why I won't be home. After I leave, I'd like you to call my brother Guthrie and tell him which things will arrive by mail and which items they'll have to go into town to pick up. A local market has agreed to deliver, but my mother or some-one has to call in the order and set up a time for the delivery to be made. I was going to discuss the changes with them this weekend, but that was before this other situation came up. They pride themselves on being self-sufficient. This will be a good time to see how they manage on their own."

"They haven't had to do anything for them-selves because you made that your job."

Coral smiled faintly. "I realized this past week that that wasn't going to work anymore. I liked being needed by them. I liked knowing there was something I could do better than they could."

"But now someone needs you just for yourself alone."

"I like to think so." She stood. "Enough of this brooding. I have a plane to catch."

"One more thing, boss."

"What's that?"

"I looked it up in *DeBrett's Correct Forms.* You're supposed to call Paul's father, Lord Denton-Forge and his mother, Lady Denton-Forge."

"Good grief," Coral muttered. "I wonder if I'm expected to curtsy."

TEN

When Paul had said that his mother and sister wouldn't be able to cope very well, Coral hadn't understood how literally he had meant that.

For the first two days she was at Tysdale Abbey, she didn't see his mother, who had been sedated by the local doctor shortly after she and Paul's father crossed the threshold of the Abbey. The Earl of Tysdale had been courteous to Coral, but distracted by his wife's health during the few encounters Coral had with the man. He spent most of his time in the master bedroom with his wife, which Coral found endearing.

She didn't take any offense when she noticed Paul's father giving her an occasional odd glance. He had every reason to wonder about her presence at Tysdale Abbey when the only explanation she'd given was that Paul had asked her to come.

Perhaps if he hadn't been preoccupied with his wife's condition, he would have questioned her relationship with his son. Once Paul's mother was feeling stronger, Coral expected the Earl to investigate why Paul had asked her to be with his family at this time.

She had no idea what to expect from Paul's mother. The possibility existed that she might not even meet the woman during her visit. Coral learned from the housekeeper and from friends who called that Mary Denton-Forge was a staunch advocate for animal rights and campaigned vigorously to prevent medical experiments being done on innocent animals. But she was not strong and brave when it came to the possibility of her children being hurt in any way. Because Lady Denton-Forge also had a heart condition, the local physician thought it a wise precaution to keep the older woman resting as much as possible.

Bouts of crying and a nasty case of morning sickness were responsible for Lindsay spending a great deal of her time in her bedroom as well. The doctor didn't recommend sedating Lindsay because of her pregnancy. He did give her something for the nausea, but that did nothing to combat her fear for Reggie and Paul's safety.

Taylor paced, worried, and poked billiard balls around a table in the game room when he wasn't with Lindsay or riding one of the estate horses.

Coral could sympathize with his feeling of helplessness. The waiting was like water dripping on a stone, slowly wearing away their patience and their nerves.

Every time the phone rang, Coral's heart stuck in her throat, and she answered with a great deal of trepidation, afraid of what the person on the other end of the line might say if it was a call from Switzerland. Mostly the people who phoned were friends and neighbors and business associates who had heard about the accident and wanted to offer their fervent best wishes for Reggie's safety. Not many were aware that Paul had joined the search party.

Coral handled most of the phone calls to spare the family the task of talking to well-meaning but occasionally tactless callers who would only distress the members of the Denton-Forge family even more. She also dealt with the newspaper reporters, who wanted to know just about everything about everyone, particularly Reggie and Paul, who, rumor had it, was tearing the mountain apart searching for his brother.

Naturally the people calling wanted to know who she was. Even after she gave her name, they were no wiser and just as curious, but Coral didn't go into detail other than to state that she was a friend of the family helping out at this time.

A few insensitive callers referred to Reggie in the past tense, which infuriated Coral. She would remind the person that the chances were just as good that Reggie would be found alive. During one of those phone calls Paul's father happened to be passing the morning room, where she had taken the call, and heard her.

She was nearly rude to the caller and was startled when she looked up and saw the Earl standing in the doorway. He clearly had heard every word she'd said.

She was astonished when he announced, "Some people are as useful as a chocolate teapot."

She had to cover the mouthpiece as she giggled at his comment and was pleased to see Paul's father smile for the first time since she'd arrived. His amused expression, however, was the mirror image of Paul's, and her heart wrenched with the fear that she might never see Paul smile in that same way again.

When she'd first met Sterling Denton-Forge, Coral had been taken aback by the remarkable physical resemblance between Paul and his father. The older man was tall and lean, his posture impeccable as was his style of dressing in slacks, shirts, and pullover sweaters, occasionally with a coat depending on the weather. His dark hair was streaked with gray, attesting to the passing of the years.

The Earl of Tysdale was, to the last ounce of his being, a gentleman, she discovered. He never once questioned her right to be there and to basically take over. He did not stand on ceremony with her, nor expect any deference from her regarding his position. He in no way made her feel she was not welcome.

The housekeeper, Mrs. Mathis, provided meals on time and kept perpetual pots of tea at the ready. Along with the housekeeper, there was plenty of staff in the house to clean and take care of the daily chores. Coral was thankful she wasn't needed to pitch in to keep the Abbey running smoothly, since she had no experience with such a large establishment.

Considering that the Abbey had ten bedrooms, Coral was surprised to be given Paul's room. She suspected Lindsay might have had something to do with that decision. Whatever the reason, being in Paul's quarters was both an agony and a comfort. Some of the mementos dated back to his childhood, giving her a picture of a younger Paul who had kept a cheap plastic trophy from winning the most coconuts at a "Coconut Shy," apparently a game or a competition of some kind. The sports equipment in one of the wardrobes wasn't a surprise. She would have been amazed not to have found any.

The people in some of the framed photographs displayed on one wall and sitting on his desk were examples of how different their lives had been. She had met a fair share of professors, scientists, and inventors, but she'd never had her picture taken while standing in knee-high water next to the Prince of Wales examining a fish one of them had caught.

When she went to bed, she put on one of his shirts to sleep in. Wearing an item of his and lying in his bed, she felt comforted and confident that he would return safely.

At nine o'clock every evening one of the coordinators of the rescue team would phone Tysdale Abbey and give an updated report of the search, which had been radioed to him from the rescue team itself.

On the third day the report was not good. Radio contact with the rescue team had been lost. They had no idea what was going on up on the mountain.

Paul's father usually took this call, and Coral and Taylor instantly knew something was wrong by the older man's expression. When the Earl poured a tot of brandy in three glasses after completing the call, Taylor and Coral exchanged worried glances before accepting their portion of the bracing drink.

When the Earl conveyed the message, Taylor murmured, "How are we going to tell Lindsay and her mother?"

Coral looked at Paul's father, who had taken his customary chair and was staring into his glass. When he didn't speak, she offered her opinion. "I know it isn't my place to tell either of you what to do, but why upset them needlessly when we don't really know what's happened? No communication from the rescue team could be because of a number of reasons that don't necessarily mean they are lost or injured or worse."

"Like what?" Taylor asked skeptically.

"The radio could have frozen, or been broken, or the batteries gone dead, or it might have fallen into a ravine. The team could be busy shoveling Reggie and his friends out of a bank of snow and don't have time to chat on the radio. There could be a dozen reasons, and none of them have to mean we give up hope."

Her discourse would have been more forceful if her voice hadn't wavered at the end. She followed the Earl's example and looked into her brandy glass rather than meet either of the men's eyes.

"You're quite right," the Earl said stoutly. "We'll proceed on the supposition that no news is good news. Paul will be operating on the theory that Reggie is alive, and that would be his priority. He will find a way to contact us when he can. In the meantime we keep this latest message to ourselves. Upsetting Lindsay and Mary at this time is premature."

Taylor and Coral nodded in agreement and silently sipped their brandy. Deep in their own thoughts, no one spoke for a long time, then Coral put her glass down.

"I doubt if any of us will sleep much tonight. Would either of you like to play cards or a game? I was up in the nursery earlier and found several puzzles, a stack of games, and some playing cards."

The Earl looked at her over his glass. "You were in the nursery?"

In case he might think she was snooping around his home, she explained, "I asked Lindsay to show me where she and her brothers spent a lot of their time when they were growing up and where the baby would stay during visits." She looked at Taylor. "I thought it might help her to keep her mind off the present by thinking of the future."

Taylor nodded. "It did help. She was in better spirits tonight when I took her dinner up to her. She even ate more than she had the last couple of days."

"She showed me the dollhouse that Paul had made into a barracks for his collection of soldiers." Coral smiled. "It sounds like him, doesn't it? He charges ahead no matter what might be in his way." She turned to Paul's father. "That's why I know he's all right and that he'll find his brother. He won't give up."

"You love my son very much, don't you, Coral?"

Coral paused while she debated how much to reveal. Finally she said, "I could deny it out of principle, but I'm not a very good liar. Yes, I am in love with Paul." She smiled again. "That's another reason he'd better get himself and his brother back here safe and sound."

Paul's father smiled in return and nodded. "With incentive like that, I have no doubts he will be home before much longer with his brother in tow. I don't believe any of us have stated our appreciation for your help through this trying time, Coral. Mary hopes to feel stronger tomorrow and wants to meet you to thank you personally for your assistance. None of us have been up to coping with the outside world just now."

Taylor added his thanks. "Lindsay doesn't feel so guilty being indisposed knowing you're taking care of things. We would like to add our appreciation for all you've done as well."

Shaking her head, she brushed off their gratitude. "I wish there was more I could do."

"Short of getting a spade and joining the search, we are all relegated to wait for news," the Earl said. "I wonder if that isn't the hardest part." He set his glass down. "I have learned the rules to a quite lively American card game from some friends of ours in France. Why don't we play a few hands to pass the time?"

Coral glanced at Taylor. "Do you feel like playing for a while? It might help."

Taylor shrugged. "Why not? Lindsay's asleep, and I'm sick of billiards."

He and Coral joined the Earl at a small round table at one side of the room, which was easily cleared of the bric-a-brac sitting on it. Paul's father took a deck of cards from a drawer built into the table and began to shuffle them with more than an amateur's skill.

Watching him manipulate the cards, Coral asked, "What is the name of this game?"

"Poker. We'll start off with five-card stud, nothing wild, jacks or better."

The terminology tripped off the older man's tongue with easy familiarity.

Coral looked at Taylor. "I think we're in trouble here."

Taylor smiled. "Now we know how he spends his time in his villa in France."

Smiling, the Earl reached over to the shelf unit next to him and took down a brass container of matches. "Let's make this interesting," he said.

Coral watched Paul's father count out an equal number of matches for each of them. She scooped her share into her hand and piled them in front of her. Her supply looked fairly puny.

Two hours later she had a more respectable stockpile. In fact she had won every matchstick that had belonged to Taylor and the Earl.

But she received much more satisfaction from knowing both men had managed to relax for a couple of hours, at least more than they had been able to before. During the last thirty minutes they had disguised several yawns behind their hands, and the hauntedness and tension of the last several days didn't appear to lie as heavily on their shoulders.

Just before midnight Taylor decided to go check on his wife and try to sleep himself. The Earl also pushed back his chair, but he made no move to leave the room until Taylor had said good night and gone upstairs.

Coral was putting the matches back in their original container when the Earl said, "You should also rest if you can."

"I will. In a while. I thought of looking through some of the books you have here in the library, if you wouldn't mind."

"Of course not. Take whatever you want." He stood and walked toward the door. "Do try to get some sleep. Staying awake won't bring them back any quicker."

"I know. I'll look for a boring book that will put me to sleep after only a few pages."

Two hours later Coral was still sitting in the library in a chair near the glowing embers of what remained of the burning coal in the fireplace, an open book on her lap. Physically she was tired, but her mind wouldn't shut down enough for her to consider it at all worthwhile going upstairs.

It wasn't the book's fault that she was unable to sleep. She had chosen a title that implied the contents would guarantee drowsiness after the first page: *The Beginner's Companion to Physics.*

She hadn't been able to concentrate on the first sentence, much less the entire first page.

All she could think about was Paul.

In a very short period of time he'd made such a difference in her life. She felt fuller, richer, more competent, less driven, more feminine and attractive. And greedy to have it all: a man who loved her and traveled on occasions, several children with skinned knees and braces, car pools, PTA meetings, and her business, plus continuing to help her parents.

As soon as Paul came back, they were going to discuss some of those things.

He had to come back first.

She was so deep in her thoughts, she jumped when the phone on the desk rang twice in succession, as British phones did. What was unusual was the time it was ringing.

It was two o'clock in the morning.

Only very important phone calls came at that hour, usually bad news, she thought, a lump of fear lodging in her chest. Then again, it could be the rescue team finally reporting in.

The physics book fell to the floor as she stood and walked quickly across the carpeted floor to grab the phone. Her heart was beating so loudly in her ears and the static was so incredibly bad on the line, she had difficulty hearing who was calling.

Then she heard her name.

"Coral?"

She closed her eyes as relief rushed through her in a flood so powerful, she thought she might be swept away by it. She sank down on the chair behind the desk, holding the receiver so tightly, her knuckles were white.

"Paul! Are you all right?"

"I'm fine."

"Reggie?" she asked, holding her breath.

"He has a broken leg, but otherwise I think he's okay. He's being checked over now. We just returned to the rescue headquarters from the base camp, so we haven't had time to do much other than get medical treatment for him and one of his friends."

She had to strain to hear what he was saying since the connection was so poor. "What about the other friend?"

"He didn't make it." Changing the subject abruptly, he asked, "How is everything there?"

"Everyone will be fine now that they know you and Reggie are all right. When can you come home?"

"Soon."

Static on the line prevented her from hearing what he said next. "I can't hear you, Paul. What did you say?"

"I've had a lot of time to think."

"About what?"

"I was wrong to ask you to move in with me."

Stunned, Coral asked, "Why?"

"We'll talk about it when I get back."

He said something else that she didn't catch. "Paul? Paul!" The crackling noises on the line hurt her ears. "I can't hear you," she yelled.

"Miss you."

She could only make out a few other garbled sounds before the line went dead completely. Giving up, she put the receiver down.

For a few minutes she didn't move from the chair. His family needed to know that Paul and Reggie were alive and basically unharmed except for Reggie's broken leg. She would wake the household and announce the good news.

For it was good news, the best news. Both men had survived and were coming home.

But Paul had also said he'd done a lot of thinking and had decided he shouldn't have asked her to move in with him. Where did that leave her except at Tysdale Abbey under false pretenses?

Right now it didn't matter what her personal situation was. The family had a right to know the news as soon as possible that Reggie and Paul would be coming home.

And she needed to pack.

Coral wasn't able to book a flight back to the States until the second day following Paul's call. It was irritating to have to wait and heartbreaking to have to pretend she was the same as she'd been before his phone call.

She'd awakened the household starting with the housekeeper, who had personally banged on the appropriate doors and shouted the news that the boys were alive. It was exactly what Coral would have done if she had known which doors to pound on. Mrs. Mathis was practically giddy with excitement as she announced that Paul had talked to Miss Coral and that he and Reggie would be home soon.

Naturally there were questions to be answered as the family gathered in the master bedroom, where Lady Mary could hear every detail of the phone call that Coral had received.

It was the first time Coral had met Paul's mother, and she saw immediately why Paul and his father were so protective of her. She was a petite woman with frail features and disposition, although the relief and love glowing in her eyes were enormous. She and Lindsay had a good cry together; this time the tears were from joy, not fear.

The Earl sent for champagne from the wine cellar, and the rescue was toasted heartily by the small group. Feeling like an intruder, Coral tried to excuse herself several times, but the Earl and Lindsay particularly wouldn't allow her to go until she'd had some champagne.

The group broke up finally, and everyone

was able to get the first sound night's sleep since Reggie had been reported missing.

Except for Coral. She packed her belongings in Paul's bedroom and bath and spent the remaining few hours of the night planning what she would do when it was daylight. Calling an airline was her first priority.

When she learned she couldn't leave until the following day, she asked the housekeeper to be shown to another bedroom, since Paul would be returning soon and would want to use his own room.

Somehow the news had gotten out quickly that the Denton-Forge heir had been found and would be returning home soon with his brother, who had been part of the search party. The Earl gave Coral a list of people he would talk to personally if they phoned, but all others not on his list she was to deal with, including the press. She kept neat, precise records of everyone who phoned and what their messages were. Luckily there were a sizable number, which kept her busy and didn't give her much time to think.

When Reggie himself phoned the Abbey from Switzerland, the Earl happened to be the one nearest the phone and answered it. Elation filled his voice when he asked Coral to alert Lindsay and Reggie's mother so that they could talk to him also.

Once she had fulfilled his request, Coral

made her way down a long hallway to a side door that led to a small garden that had been landscaped with topiary trees and an extensive rose garden, still in flower. The lawn was manicured perfectly, adding to the tranquillity of the spot.

Coral barely noticed any of her surroundings. She was happy for the family, she honestly was, but the feeling of being left out, of not belonging, lingered like a nagging shadow that wouldn't go away. Paul's family wasn't at fault. She had introduced herself as a friend of Paul's and had been treated with the utmost kindness and consideration because of that status.

While she was sitting on one of the hard iron chairs, the Earl stepped out of the side door and looked around. When he spotted her, he walked over to where she was sitting.

"Here you are. We sent Mrs. Mathis to look for you in the house. Reggie wanted to talk to you."

"Why would Reggie want to talk to me?" she asked, startled. "He doesn't even know me."

"Reg probably knows all about you from Paul. They have always shared confidences since they were young." He gave her a sharp, searching glance. "I don't want you to take this the wrong way, but it's important that you are aware of Paul's close ties to his family. I hope you don't resent that in any way."

"Of course not. I'm very close to my parents, and I have two brothers of my own. Over the years they've teased me unmercifully about one thing or another, but were always there when I needed them." Remembering Guthrie's hug and Latin quotation, she added, "And they still are."

"Good," the Earl said firmly. "Anyone involved with Paul will need to understand his feelings for his whole family. His roots go very deep in history as well as in English soil. His children will be part of that proud heritage."

Coral tilted her head slightly as she studied Paul's father. "I've heard that it's possible for an American to be told off by an English gentleman without realizing he's been insulted. Is this one of those times? Am I being warned off? If that's the case, you can stop worrying, my lord. Paul and I have been seeing each other only a couple of weeks. He has made me no promises or commitments, so you and your family can relax. I won't be soiling the Denton-Forge linen."

It was the Earl's turn to be startled. "You've completely misunderstood me, Coral. I meant no insult whatsoever. The fact that you are here at Paul's behest tells us a great deal about his involvement with you." He smiled. "Perhaps there might have been a small amount of warning in what I was saying in that you should know what you're getting into with Paul's background."

Coral looked away. "I understand."

She hadn't meant to speak so flatly, but she had, and the Earl couldn't help hearing the bitterness in her voice.

"Time will show you we are not quite as imposing as you might think," he said. "Paul gave us their flight time tomorrow so we thought we would all descend on the airport en masse to bid them welcome. Mary even feels strong enough to make the trip. Lindsay has insisted on joining us. You'll come as well of course."

Evading his command, she asked, "What time will their plane be landing?"

He quoted the time Paul had given him, and told her they would be leaving the Abbey at ten in the morning in order to get there in plenty of time.

Paul and Reggie's flight would be landing thirty minutes before her flight to the States was scheduled to depart. She had planned on hiring a car to take her to the airport, which would be easier and less stressful than explaining why she would want to take her luggage with her if she rode with the Denton-Forges and the Ellisons.

"I'll let you know in the morning what my plans are."

The Earl's expression clearly showed he did not like her vague answer. "Are you feeling well, Coral? I realize you have been under a great deal of stress, as we all have, plus you've been dealing with the outside world for us. We can call the physician if you need treatment of some kind."

Coral's immediate reaction was to say her health was fine, but she realized not feeling well would be a good excuse not to go to the airport with them. Then she could go ahead on her own and fly back home.

"It's not necessary for me to see a doctor. I think it's just that I haven't been sleeping very well, and I have a slight headache. We've all been under a great deal of strain. Now that we know Reggie and Paul are safe, things can get back to normal."

Paul's father didn't look reassured. "If you change your mind about seeing our physician, you need only say the word and we'll call him."

Coral's plans to fake an illness were unnecessary, though. Paul phoned again just before his flight took off the next morning with a warning that the press would undoubtedly be at Heathrow Airport when he and Reggie arrived, just as they'd been pestering them since the rescue. He told his father to tell Coral not to come to the airport because of the publicity.

Coral surprised herself by not taking the message from Paul in a negative way. She wasn't as sure of him as she would like, but she knew instinctively that he wouldn't purposely hurt her by implying he didn't want their relationship publicized. She preferred to think he remembered her reaction to the spotlight at Montego Qui's concert and wanted to spare her feelings.

In fact during the night she'd done a lot of thinking and had decided Paul was going to have to tell her in person what he'd meant by his remark that he shouldn't have asked her to move in with him.

She wasn't going to run back to the States without knowing for sure that they either had a chance for something permanent or it was over. She could deal with sure things. It was the *if*s and *maybe*s that were driving her crazy.

After Paul's family left for the airport, Coral was too restless just to sit quietly with a magazine or a book while she waited. She couldn't bear to sit at all. She wandered from room to room and back again until she was getting sour glances from the housekeeper and the two maids, who were scurrying around with dust rags and vases of fresh flowers before the sons returned.

With a small amount of exasperation Mrs. Mathis hinted that one of the Earl's farm dogs had recently given birth to a litter of puppies. If Miss Coral wished to see them, they were in the stables, which was a little ways to walk but would be well worth the trek.

And well out of the housekeeper's way, thought Coral as she headed toward the long stone-and-wood building pointed out to her by one of the gardeners. Small pebbles of gravel crunched pleasantly under her shoes as she strolled with her hands in the pockets of the loden-green cloth jacket she wore over a white shirt tucked into tan pleated slacks.

The peace and tranquillity of the estate seeped into her as she walked along. Birds were calling to one another in the trees, but that was the only sound Coral heard. She visualized Paul's ancestors walking where she was stepping and thought about what his father had said about respecting Paul's background and accepting it as an important part of his life.

Where he came from was part of who Paul was, the same as her family was the base from which she had formed the person she was today. She didn't want to deny his background or her own.

His past wasn't a problem for her. The present and the future, on the other hand, were of very deep concern to her.

The puppies were being kept in a corner of an empty stall. Coral approached cautiously, talking quietly to the mother, who watched her, her head down over several nursing bundles of fur. Coral guessed that the mother was a combination of several breeds of canines, though the look of the sleek black-and-white dogs that helped herd sheep was the prevalent characteristic.

She sat down on some straw several feet away and leaned back against the side of the stall. The clean smell of the bedding blended with the more pungent aroma of horses. She continued talking to the mother in a calm voice and was rewarded by the dog gradually raising her head, no longer as protective of her brood when Coral didn't appear to pose a threat.

When one of the puppies ambled over in her direction, Coral put out her hand for him to sniff. Soon she had all five of them climbing over her legs and licking her face with little tails wagging. The mother looked on indulgently as Coral played with her offspring.

Unaware of the passage of time, Coral nearly dropped one of the puppies when a familiar male voice spoke from several feet away.

"Of all the ways I pictured you while I was gone, rolling about in the hay wasn't one of them."

The puppies were dislodged from their playground as Coral sprang up and threw herself into the arms of the man standing at the stall entrance.

Paul's arms closed around her so tightly, she could hardly breathe, but she didn't mind. She was holding him with all of her strength. In between kissing him she asked questions, yet didn't give him any time to answer them.

Paul kissed her deeply and for a very long

time, effectively cutting off all inquiries as to his health, his brother, and the rescue itself.

When kisses weren't enough, and he realized anything else was impossible, Paul lifted his head and cupped her face between his warm palms.

"I missed you too," he said softly.

The sound of the puppies whining for attention made Coral smile. "We're disturbing the kids."

"They'll have to adjust. This might be the only time I can be alone with you until tonight, so I'm going to take advantage of it. Reggie is anxious to meet you, and I'll never get a word in once he starts up. If he hadn't been on crutches, I wouldn't have been able to get you to myself even now."

Even though she was happy to see him, she couldn't stop the tears from welling up in her eyes.

Paul looked horrified. "What are you crying for? It's all over, and Reggie and I are back safe and sound."

"I was so scared. I can sympathize with Victoria more than I could when I met her. If she worries like I have the past several days, no wonder she doesn't want John to go jumping off of cliffs anymore."

With his thumb Paul brushed away one of the tears that slowly trailed down her cheek.

"Now I know why John could give it up. When you love someone, you don't want to hurt her."

Coral stared at him. Blinking away the tears, she asked, "What did you say?"

"I said I can understand how John could give up the adventurous life."

"Not that part. The other part."

A corner of his mouth lifted slightly, his eyes sparkling with amusement and a great deal of tenderness. "What part?"

"You know darn well what part. About loving someone and not wanting to hurt her."

"What about it?"

Coral realized that behind Paul's teasing was a vulnerability she should have recognized before. She saw it in her own reflection. He wasn't sure of her feelings for him any more than she knew what his had been for her.

"Your father warned me that anyone involved with you would have to respect your background. He even implied that your children would be part of that history."

"The hell he did!"

"Don't be angry with him. He was right. The same as anyone involved with me would have to understand how protective I am of my family. But even more important than either one of those requirements, the man I'm involved with has to love me as much as I love him. And . . . Paul! What are you doing?"

"I'm kissing you, so will you kindly hush a moment?"

She didn't mind at all. Maybe after about a hundred more kisses just like that one, she'd be able to forget the terror of the last couple of days.

The need for air and control made Paul break away from her mouth and bury his face in her neck.

"Paul?" she murmured.

"Hmmm?"

"What did you mean when you said on the phone that you were wrong to ask me to move in with you?"

He raised his head. "I should have asked you to marry me instead. I realized I should have asked you the first day I stormed into your office."

"You were angry with me!"

"Darn right. And I will be again if you organize my office in any way, shape, or form in our lifetime. You keep tidying up the world if you want to, darling. Just leave my corner of it the way I like it. Is that a deal?"

She nodded. "And when you go away on your scouting trips, you will be extra careful you don't do anything really stupid and get hurt or worse?"

"After we speed up your training schedule, you'll be in shape to come with me on some of the trips." He grinned when she groaned. "But after the children come, we'll both make adjustments to our work schedules."

The puppies tumbled over the tops of their shoes and scrambled for attention, but it did them no good. The two people were much more interested in each other than they were in them.

THE EDITOR'S CORNER

Wrap up your summer in the most romantic way with the four upcoming LOVESWEPTs. Chivalry is alive and well in these love stories, so get ready for the most delicious thrills as each of the heroines finds her knight in shining armor.

Beloved for stories that weave heartbreak and humor into a tapestry of unforgettable romance, Helen Mittermeyer opens this month with **DYNASTY JONES,** LOVESWEPT #754. She is beautiful, spirited, a flame-haired angel whose lips promise heaven, but Aaron Burcell has to discover why his missing racehorse is grazing in Dynasty Jones's pasture! Honeysuckle Farm has been her sanctuary until Aaron breaches the walls that keep her safe from sorrow. Dynasty awakens every passionate impulse Aaron has ever felt, makes him want to slay dragons, but he must make her believe he will not betray her trust. Immerse yourself in this moving and tender tale of a love that heals with sweet and tender fire by the ever-popular Helen Mittermeyer.

Catch **ROGUE FEVER**, LOVESWEPT #755 by Jan Hudson. Long legs in dusty jeans, eyes shaded by a cowboy hat, Ben Favor looks every inch a scoundrel—and Savanna Smith feels his smile as a kiss of fire on her skin! She'd come to the sleepy Mexican town to trace a con man, but her search keeps getting sidetracked by a mesmerizing devil who makes her burn, then fans the flames. Savanna is the kind of woman a man will walk through fire for, but Ben will have to battle charging bulls and bad guys just to call this teasing temptress his. Award-winning Jan Hudson escorts you south of the border where the smart and sassy heroine always gets her man.

No city sizzles like New Orleans in Faye Hughes' **GOTTA HAVE IT**, LOVESWEPT #756. Once he'd been the most notorious jewel thief in the world, stealing from the rich for charity's sake, but now Remy Ballou insists he's gone straight—and Michael Ann O'Donnell fears for the legendary gems she's been hired to protect! His rogue's grin has haunted her dreams, while memories of his caresses still heat her blood. His words make her burn and his touch makes her shiver, but will the pirate who captured her soul long ago bind his heart to hers forever, or vanish in the shadows of the night? Find out in this steamy, sultry love story from Faye Hughes.

Debra Dixon explores the dangerous passions that spark between dusk and dawn in **HOT AS SIN**, LOVESWEPT #757. Emily Quinn is on the run, desperate to disappear before anyone else loses his life to save hers—and Gabe is her only hope! Tempted by her mystery, he agrees to help her evade her pursuers, but hiding a woman whose nightmares draw him into the line of fire awaken yearnings in his own secret heart. Once Gabe becomes more than a safe place to run, Emily strives to show him that forever will not be long enough. Let Debra Dixon lead you through this darkly sensual and exquisitely potent story about risking everything for love.

Happy reading!

With warmest wishes,

Beth de Guzman   Shauna Summers

Senior Editor   Associate Editor

P.S. Watch for these spectacular Bantam women's fiction titles coming in September: With **LORD OF THE DRAGON,** Suzanne Robinson, one of the reigning stars of historical romance, presents her latest captivating love story in which a willful beauty and a vengeful knight cross swords; winner of the Catherine Cookson Prize for Fiction, Susanna Kearsley debuts as a spectacular new talent with **MARIANA,** a suspenseful tale of time travel that may be one of the most hauntingly beautiful love stories of the year. See next month's LOVESWEPTs for a preview of these enticing novels. And immediately following this page, look for a preview of the wonderful romances from Bantam that are *available now!*

Don't miss these extraordinary books
by your favorite Bantam authors

On sale in July:

DEFIANT
by Patricia Potter

STARCROSSED
by Susan Krinard

BEFORE I WAKE
by Terry Lawrence

DEFIANT

by "master storyteller"*
Patricia Potter

Only the desire for vengeance had spurred Wade Foster on, until the last of the men who had destroyed his family lay sprawled on the dirt. Now, badly wounded, the rugged outlaw closed his eyes against the pain . . . and awoke to the tender touch of the one woman who could show him how to live—and love—again.

"He'll be all right now, won't he?" her son asked.

Mary Jo nodded. "I think so. At least, I think he'll live. I don't know about that arm."

Jeff frowned. "Do you think he might be a lawman?"

"No," she said gently, "I don't think so."

"He wore his gun tied down."

"A lot of men wear their guns tied down."

"Did he say anything to you?"

She shook her head. She hated lying to her son, but she didn't want to tell him his new acquaintance had so coldly said he'd killed three men.

"Maybe he's a marshal. Or an army scout. He was wearing Indian beads."

"I don't think so, Jeff," she said. "He could just be a drifter."

"Then why did someone shoot him? Did he say?"

She shook her head, telling herself it wasn't a lie.

* *Rendezvous*

Wade Foster hadn't explained exactly why he'd been shot.

"Can I go see him?"

"I think he needs a little privacy right now," Mary Jo said. "But as soon as those biscuits are done, you can take some in and see if he can eat them."

Jeff was scuffing his shoes on the floor, waiting impatiently for the biscuits. She sought a way to expel some of that energy. "Why don't you get some wood for the fireplace?"

He nodded, fetched his oilcloth slicker, and disappeared out the door, eager for some action, even if it was only doing chores. She was hoping there would be a school next year; currently, there weren't enough families to support one, and she'd been teaching him herself from the few books she'd been able to find.

She stirred the broth as she kept her ears open for sounds beyond her bedroom door. Wade Foster should be finished with his personal needs now. He would need a wash and a shave.

She'd occasionally shaved her husband. It was one of the few personal things he'd enjoyed having done for him. But she hesitated to offer that service to the stranger. It had been an intimate thing between her and her husband; they had even occasionally ended in bed, though he usually preferred night for lovemaking. In some ways, he had been prudish about lovemaking, feeling there was a time and place for it, while Mary Jo thought any place or time was right between husband and wife as long as the desire was there.

The thought brought a hot blush to her cheeks and a yearning to her womanly place. It had been nearly three years since she'd last been loved. Hard work had subdued the need but now she felt the rush of heat deep inside.

She shook her head in disgust at herself. She couldn't believe she was having such feelings for the first stranger that came limping along. Especially this stranger.

But she just plain couldn't get Wade Foster out of her mind, not those intense eyes, or that strong, lean body under her bedclothes. Perhaps because of his grief over his son. She'd known grief, but she had never lost a child. And she'd never seen a man so consumed by sorrow.

He was a very disturbing man in many ways and she was foolish to harbor him without checking with the law.

Perhaps when the storm ended, she would ride to town and make inquiries. If she could ford the stream. If—

The door banged open and Jeff plunged back inside, rain flying in with him. Jake stayed outside, barking frantically.

"Men coming, Ma," Jeff said. "A lot of them."

Is anyone after you?

I expect so.

Almost without thinking, she made a decision.

"Jeff, don't say anything about the stranger."

"Why?" It was his favorite question and she always tried to give him answers. This time she didn't know if she could.

She looked at her son, wondering what kind of lesson she was teaching him now. But she had to protect the man they'd rescued. She didn't understand why she felt so strongly about it but there it was.

She tried the truth. "I think he's in trouble but I don't think he's a bad man."

Jeff thought about the answer for a moment. It was *his* stranger after all. He had found him. Well, his dog Jake had found him. And Jake liked him. That made the stranger all right in his book.

He nodded.

Mary Jo hurried toward her bedroom, giving only a brief knock before entering without invitation.

Wade Foster was on the side of the bed, the sheet obviously pulled quickly in front of his privates. His face was drenched in sweat, the color pale, his lips clenched together.

"Men are coming," she voiced aloud. "Could be a posse."

He tried to stand but couldn't. He fell back against the pillow, swearing softly. "I don't want to bring you trouble."

"No one could know you're here. The rain would have erased any tracks," she said. "I'll turn them away."

He stared at her. "Why?"

"I don't know," she said frankly.

"I don't want you or the boy involved."

"We already are, Mr. Foster. Now just stay here and be quiet."

"I don't understand you."

Mary Jo smiled. "Not many people do."

A loud knocking came at the front door, accompanied by Jake's renewed barking. She wished she'd had time to hide Wade Foster, she would just have to make sure no one searched the house. Thank God, everyone in this area knew she was the widow of a Texas Ranger and the heir of another. She would be the last person suspected of harboring a fugitive.

Casting a reassuring look at Jeff, she hurried to

the door, opened it and faced the sheriff and six of her neighbors.

"A man was found dead, killed some four miles to the west," Sheriff Matt Sinclair said. "We're checking all the ranches and farms."

She gave him a warm smile. Since the day that she and Jeff had come to Cimarron Valley, Matt had been kind, attentive, and concerned that she was trying to run a ranch on her own. Others had been contemptuous.

"In this weather?" she asked.

"The dead man appears to be a miner from his clothing, though God only knows what he was doing here." He cleared his throat, then added reluctantly, "He was shot once in the leg and then in the throat at close range. Cold-blooded killing if I've ever seen one. Just wanted to alert everyone, check if they've seen any strangers around."

Mary Jo slowly absorbed the news. Wade Foster had tried to warn her but she hadn't been prepared for the details.

"Do you have any idea who did it?"

"That there's the devil of it," the sheriff replied. "No one's seen or heard anything. Could be just plain robbery, and the killer's long gone, but I want to be sure everyone's warned."

"Thank you," Mary Jo said.

"I don't like leaving a woman and kid alone," he said. "One of my men can stay with you, sleep in the barn."

Mary Jo shook her head. "My husband taught me to shoot as good as any man and I wouldn't be reluctant to do it," she said. "Jeff here is just as good. And Jake would warn us of any trespassers. But I thank you for the offer."

"Well, then, if everything's all right . . ." His voice trailed off.

"Thank you for coming by, Sheriff." Mary Jo knew she should offer them something, particularly coffee but it was too risky. She started to shut the door.

The sheriff added, "I'll send someone over every couple of days to check on you."

"No need."

"Just to make me feel better," he said with a slight smile.

Mary Jo tried to smile back, but couldn't. She felt terribly deceitful.

Tell him, something inside her demanded. Tell him about the murderer in your bed.

But no words came. She merely nodded her thanks. As she watched him and the others mount their horses and ride away, she wondered if she had just made the worst mistake of her life.

"Susan Krinard was born to write romance."
—*Amanda Quick*

STARCROSSED
by Susan Krinard

At sixteen, Lady Ariane Burke-Marchand had loved Rook Galloway with all the passion and pain of unrequited love. It didn't matter that the handsome Kalian was separated from her by birth and caste and mansion walls. All she knew was that this exotic, mysterious creature called to her in ways she couldn't fathom or resist. But that was eight years ago, eight years before the deadly riots that pitted Marchand against Kalian and turned the man she worshiped into an enemy she loathed. . . .

Hudson ducked his head. "Permission to examine your hold and cabins, Lady Ariane. A formality."

A breath of wry laughter escaped her. "I'm not likely to be harboring fugitives on my ship, but I'll clear you."

She led him into the cargo hold and left him there, making her way through the final air lock and into the *d'Artagnan's* living quarters. There was something almost oppressive in the empty silence of the common room; even the cockpit seemed less a sanctuary than a cell.

Ariane shuddered and dropped into the padded

pilot's seat. *Don't think about it*, she commanded herself. *At least this ship is something you can count on. Something certain.*

One by one she ran through the preflight routines: checking the stardrive's balance for sublight flight, priming the ship's life support system, carrying out all the necessary tests. Again and again she forgot sequences that she knew by heart, remembering Rook's face.

Remembering how he had made her feel. . . .

No. Her fingers trembled on the keypad as she made the final entries. *You won't have to think about it much longer. It's over. It's out of your hands.*

But the memories remained while the ready lights came up on the control panel. She leaned back in the pilot's seat and passed her hand over her face.

Honor. All her life she'd been raised by the codes of the Espérancian Elite. Like the *d'Artagnan*, honor was solid and real. It had been insanity to doubt, to question. Duty and honor would send her back to Espérance. Honor would give her the courage to face a life of confinement. To accept.

To forget Rook Galloway.

Letting out a shuddering breath, she rose and began to pace the tiny space of the cockpit restlessly. Hudson should have been done with his "routine" check by now. She flipped on the ship's intercom.

"Mr. Hudson? I'm ready for takeoff." She waited, tapping her fingers against the smooth console. "Mr. Hudson—"

"Here, Lady Ariane."

She whirled, with reflexes honed through years of training as a duelist. Hudson stood just inside the cockpit, a disruptor in his hand.

Aimed at her.

Her first impulse was to laugh. Hudson looked so deadly serious, his mouth set in a grim line that seemed so much at odds with his boyishly untouched face. But she clamped her lips together and balanced lightly on the balls of her feet, waiting.

"Did you find some—irregularity, Mr. Hudson?"

He moved another step closer. And another, until he was within touching distance. "Call for clearance to take off," he said, gesturing with the 'ruptor.

Ariane revised her first assumption. It wasn't what she had supposedly done; Hudson had simply gone crazy.

"I know—how it must be, Mr. Hudson. Alone here, far from home—you want to go back home, is that it? To Liberty?"

He stared at her, light blue eyes shadowed beneath his uniform cap. "Liberty," he repeated.

Considering the best way to move, Ariane tensed her muscles for action. "You must feel trapped here, so far from home. After what we saw . . . I understand. But—"

His smile vanished. "Trapped," he said softly. "What do you know about being trapped, Lady Ariane?" His voice had gone very deep and strange. "Call the tower for clearance. Now."

For the briefest instant Hudson's eyes flickered to the console behind her, and Ariane moved. She darted at Hudson, whirling like a dancer in the ancient way her family's old Weapons Master had taught her as a girl. She might as well have attacked a plasteel bulkhead. Powerful arms caught and held her; the 'ruptor's muzzle came up against her head.

Shock held her utterly still for one blinding instant. Hudson's hand burned on her arm like the bitter cold of space.

"I don't have much to lose, Lady Ariane," Hudson said softly. "You'll call for clearance. Everything is perfectly—normal."

She considered fighting again; to put the *d'Artagnan* in a starjacker's hands was unthinkable.

But there was far more at stake. Marchand honor and Marchand interest demanded her safe return, to wed Wynn Slayton by inviolable contract that would bind their families forever. Her death now would gain nothing at all.

Clenching her teeth, Ariane hailed the prison port and made the final, in-person request for clearance. The bored officer's voice on the other end of the commlink never altered; her own was perfectly steady as she acknowledged her clearance to lift.

Abruptly Hudson let her go. "Very good," he murmured. "Take her up."

Ariane thought quickly as she dropped into the pilot's seat, Hudson breathing harshly over her shoulder. *He's only a boy. He can't know much about Caravel-class starships. . . .*

Her hand hovered just above the control stick. It shouldn't be too difficult to fool the young guard, make it seem as if they were leaving the system. And then—

Warm fingers feathered along her shoulder and slid under the thick hair at the base of her neck. "Oh no, Lady Ariane. It won't be so easy this time."

Her throat went dry as her hand fell from the console. Abruptly he let her go, stepping away. She turned in the seat to look up at the man who stood over her.

And he *changed*. As if he were made of something other than mere human flesh he began to change:

slowly, so slowly that at first she didn't realize what she was seeing.

The young man's softness vanished, cheekbones and hollows and sharp angles drawn forth from Hudson's unremarkable face. Sandy hair darkened in a slow wave under the uniform cap. An old scar snaked over skin tanned by relentless heat.

The eyes were the last to change. Blue faded, warmed, melted into copper.

Rook's eyes.

They held hers as he swept off his cap, freed the dark hair that fell to his shoulders.

The man who stood before her wore the tailored uniform of a Tantalan guard as a hellhound might wear a collar. A wild beast crouched on the deck of the *d'Artagnan*.

A Kalian.

Reaction coursed through her, numbing her hands and stopping her breath.

"*Mon Dieu*," she whispered. "You."

BEFORE I WAKE
by Terry Lawrence

*Loveswept star Terry Lawrence is an extraordinary story-
teller whose novels sizzle with irresistible wit and high-
voltage passion. Now, she weaves the beloved fairy tale*
Sleeping Beauty *into a story so enthralling it will keep
you up long into the night. . . .*

She came clean. "Gabe, I simply must apologize. I
have something I'm sorry to tell you."

"You're married."

She croaked a laugh. "Ha ha. No." Her flippant
wave fooled no one. She wasn't good with men. Actually, she wasn't bad. She'd had relationships. Some of
them had proceeded all the way to bed and *then*
they'd fallen apart. "We taped you."

"You what?"

She swung around in her chair and retrieved the
black plastic box. When she swung back he was still
smiling. This time a cautious glint lurked in his blue
eyes.

"The night tech on duty in the sleep lab the evening you were here filmed you sleeping. It's common
practice, we do it all the time."

"Do you?"

"I'm apologizing because we didn't have your permission."

"Ah." He took the tape from her, his tapering fingers touching hers. Their gazes met and held. "Did you watch it?"

Where were those stacks of folders when she needed a place to hide? "A little. You seemed to have slept well."

"Like the dead." One side of his mouth curved up.

She'd never noticed the way his brows arched, like Gothic windows in a gloomy cathedral. He had an air of the fallen angel about him, the devilish rogue, the lost soul. He'd referred to himself as something of the sort, though she couldn't remember exactly how.

She felt light-headed. The atmosphere was too close. She'd been lost in his eyes too long. She needed air. She could handle this. She rose, her legs shaking, and edged her way around her desk. From there to the window seemed like miles.

He turned his head, following her with his eyes. His body seemed unnaturally still. Hers seemed unbearably energized. Her pulse skittered through her veins. Her breath skimmed in and out of her lungs.

"So you've been sleeping better," she said, making conversation, gripping the window frame. The wood was ancient, the paint peeling and dry. She shoved. The frame didn't budge. Pressing her wrists against the chilly glass, she tried again. Her breath frosted the pane. She inhaled the musty odor of rotting wood.

Gabe reached around her from behind. She froze, her breath trapped in her lungs. He rested his thumbs on her knuckles, splaying his hands on either side of hers. In one sharp move he thrust the window upward. The wood screeched like an angry bird.

In the ensuing silence, traffic noise rose from the street below. Cold air flooded the room, slithering into the gaps of her coat, shocking her with its icy fingers. She turned with great effort. Sagging against the sill, she gripped the splintery wood on either side of her thighs.

Gabe rested his hands on her shoulders. "Shana."

His grogginess was long gone. A feral alertness sharpened his features. He lingered over her name like a starving man over a meal. His lids lowered. He concentrated on her lips. She longed to taste his.

She fought for air, for sense. She couldn't do this. Whirling in the tight circle of his arms, she flattened her palms against the glass. They instantly formed a misty outline, ten fingers clutching thin air.

His fingers closed over her wrists like talons capturing her hammering pulse. His thumbs curled into her damp palms. Mingled breaths frosted the pane, blotting out the world outside.

"Please," she panted. She was slipping, her will ebbing with every weak breath. This wasn't right. She pressed her cheek to the window, letting the mind-clearing reality of bitter cold bite into it. The chill penetrated her clothing, pebbling her breasts. The hard line of the sill pressed across her thighs.

An eerie incongruous warmth whispered across her face. His breath. He lifted her hair off her neck. She tried to protest. Her lips barely parted. "I can't believe we're doing this again."

"Believe."

"We can't."

"We can."

And don't miss these spellbinding
romances from Bantam Books,
on sale in August:

LORD OF THE DRAGON
by Suzanne Robinson

"An author with star quality . . . spectacularly
talented."
—*Romantic Times*

MARIANA
by Susanna Kearsley

Winner of the Catherine Cookson Prize for fiction

To enter the sweepstakes outlined below, you must respond by the date specified and follow all entry instructions published elsewhere in this offer.

DREAM COME TRUE SWEEPSTAKES

Sweepstakes begins 9/1/94, ends 1/15/96. To qualify for the Early Bird Prize, entry must be received by the date specified elsewhere in this offer. Winners will be selected in random drawings on 2/29/96 by an independent judging organization whose decisions are final. Early Bird winner will be selected in a separate drawing from among all qualifying entries.

Odds of winning determined by total number of entries received. Distribution not to exceed 300 million.

Estimated maximum retail value of prizes: Grand (1) $25,000 (cash alternative $20,000); First (1) $2,000; Second (1) $750; Third (50) $75; Fourth (1,000) $50; Early Bird (1) $5,000. Total prize value: $86,500.

Automobile and travel trailer must be picked up at a local dealer; all other merchandise prizes will be shipped to winners. Awarding of any prize to a minor will require written permission of parent/guardian. If a trip prize is won by a minor, s/he must be accompanied by parent/legal guardian. Trip prizes subject to availability and must be completed within 12 months of date awarded. Blackout dates may apply. Early Bird trip is on a space available basis and does not include port charges, gratuities, optional shore excursions and onboard personal purchases. Prizes are not transferable or redeemable for cash except as specified. No substitution for prizes except as necessary due to unavailability. Travel trailer and/or automobile license and registration fees are winners' responsibility as are any other incidental expenses not specified herein.

Early Bird Prize may not be offered in some presentations of this sweepstakes. Grand through third prize winners will have the option of selecting any prize offered at level won. All prizes will be awarded. Drawing will be held at 204 Center Square Road, Bridgeport, NJ 08014. Winners need not be present. For winners list (available in June, 1996), send a self-addressed, stamped envelope by 1/15/96 to: Dream Come True Winners, P.O. Box 572, Gibbstown, NJ 08027.

THE FOLLOWING APPLIES TO THE SWEEPSTAKES ABOVE:

No purchase necessary. No photocopied or mechanically reproduced entries will be accepted. Not responsible for lost, late, misdirected, damaged, incomplete, illegible, or postage-die mail. Entries become the property of sponsors and will not be returned.

Winner(s) will be notified by mail. Winner(s) may be required to sign and return an affidavit of eligibility/release within 14 days of date on notification or an alternate may be selected. Except where prohibited by law, entry constitutes permission to use of winners' names, hometowns, and likenesses for publicity without additional compensation. Void where prohibited or restricted. All federal, state, provincial, and local laws and regulations apply.

All prize values are in U.S. currency. Presentation of prizes may vary; values at a given prize level will be approximately the same. All taxes are winners' responsibility.

Canadian residents, in order to win, must first correctly answer a time-limited skill testing question administered by mail. Any litigation regarding the conduct and awarding of a prize in this publicity contest by a resident of the province of Quebec may be submitted to the Regie des loteries et courses du Quebec.

Sweepstakes is open to legal residents of the U.S., Canada, and Europe (in those areas where made available) who have received this offer.

Sweepstakes in sponsored by Ventura Associates, 1211 Avenue of the Americas, New York, NY 10036 and presented by independent businesses. Employees of these, their advertising agencies and promotional companies involved in this promotion, and their immediate families, agents, successors, and assignees shall be ineligible to participate in the promotion and shall not be eligible for any prizes covered herein. SWP 3/95

DON'T MISS THESE FABULOUS BANTAM WOMEN'S FICTION TITLES

On sale in July

DEFIANT
by PATRICIA POTTER
Winner of the 1992 *Romantic Times*
Career Achievement Award for Storyteller of the Year

Only the desire for vengeance had spurred Wade Foster on, until the last of the men who had destroyed his family lay sprawled in the dirt. Now, badly wounded, the rugged outlaw closed his eyes against the pain . . . and awoke to the tender touch of the one woman who could show him how to live— and love—again. _____ 56601-6 $5.50/$6.99

STAR-CROSSED
by nationally bestselling author SUSAN KRINARD

"Susan Krinard was born to write romance."
—New York Times *bestselling author Amanda Quick*

A captivating futuristic romance in the tradition of Johanna Lindsey, Janelle Taylor, and Kathleen Morgan. A beautiful aristocrat risks a forbidden love . . . with a dangerously seductive man born of an alien race. _____ 56917-1 $4.99/$5.99

BEFORE I WAKE
by TERRY LAWRENCE

"Terry Lawrence is a magnificent writer." —Romantic Times
Award-winning author Terry Lawrence is an extraordinary storyteller whose novels sizzle with irresistible wit and high-voltage passion. Now, she weaves the beloved fairy tale *Sleeping Beauty* into a story so enthralling it will keep you up long into the night. _____ 56914-7 $5.50/$6.99

Ask for these books at your local bookstore or use this page to order.

Please send me the books I have checked above. I am enclosing $_____ (add $2.50 to cover postage and handling). Send check or money order, no cash or C.O.D.'s, please.

Name _____

Address _____

City/State/Zip _____

Send order to: Bantam Books, Dept. FN159, 2451 S. Wolf Rd., Des Plaines, IL 60018
Allow four to six weeks for delivery.

Prices and availability subject to change without notice. FN 159 7/95